THE PARALLEL STORIES OF
JOSEPH & JESUS

To our good friends
Zolan + Parson

Grady

THE PARALLEL STORIES OF

JOSEPH & JESUS

GRADY LAXSON

Pleasant Word
A Division of WINEPRESS PUBLISHING

Pleasant Word (a division of WinePress Publishing, PO Box 428, Enumclaw, WA 98022) functions only as book publisher. As such, the ultimate design, content, editorial accuracy, and views expressed or implied in this work are those of the author.

Unless otherwise noted, all Scriptures are taken from the Holy Bible, New International Version, Copyright © 1973, 1978, 1984 by the International Bible Society. Used by permission of Zondervan Publishing House. The "NIV" and "New International Version" trademarks are registered in the United States Patent and Trademark Office by International Bible Society.

Scripture references marked KJV are taken from the King James Version of the Bible.

Scripture references marked NASB are taken from the New American Standard Bible, © 1960, 1963, 1968, 1971, 1972, 1973, 1975, 1977 by The Lockman Foundation. Used by permission.

ISBN 1-4141-0453-7
Library of Congress Catalog Card Number: 2005903531

Contents

Introduction

C.H. Roland, a fictional character, had an out-of-body experience. While paramedics worked on his drowned body, he followed an angel through Canaan and Egypt. He looked through the open door into heaven alongside the apostle John and ended up with the apostles on the day of Pentecost.

God was answering C.H.'s prayer. He had asked God to help him know Jesus because he wanted to write about Him.

C.H. was able to personally witness the story of Joseph and to identify many points of congruency between the stories of the two men who lived thirty-nine generations apart. He became obsessed with desire for the Bread of Heaven.

The stories of Joseph and Jesus are parallel stories, and the points of congruency reveal the amazing signs and wonders of God. It should be clear to any open-minded person that Jesus is God's Son.

While the book is a novel, it required much research, and it strives to cling very tightly to Scripture. Doctrinal arguments that may arise from the book will not be with the author; they will be with God and His signs.

A Dead Man

Good grief," exclaimed C.H., astounded at what he was seeing. "Would you look at that?" He peered down at the small crowd gathered on the edge of the lake. Paramedics were hovering over a man's body, trying to pump water out of his lungs and resuscitate him.

C.H. recognized himself lying on the ground. "That's me," he shouted. "I'm…I'm out of my body!" He looked more closely at his slack, wet, disheveled body being pummeled by the medical technicians. He could hear people talking. Someone was yelling on a cell phone.

"That's me down there," he said. "How can I be down—" He paused, confused at being in two places. He poked himself. He felt his face. "What the heck? I'm up here."

After a moment of watching things on the ground, C.H. said, "I guess I drowned. That sorry boat! I should have fished from the shore."

Then the thought hit him like a bolt. "My gosh! Am I dead? Oh, no! I must be dead."

Frustrated with his job as a journalist, C. H. Roland had taken the day off and headed for Lynx Lake to do a little fishing. He needed a break.

He had written articles about fishing from a canoe, but had no personal experience with such a craft. He thought it sounded like fun. And since being careful was not his style, he manned the canoe with gusto.

C.H. lived life in a geared-up mode, always searching for sensational stories. He seethed with frustration every day, trying to break the news on something big. A craven desire drove him hard.

In spite of his rowdy, profane nature, and speech peppered with down-home slang and expletives, his assignment from the newspaper editor was to cover social clubs and churches. A misfit if there ever was one.

"And I don't want dull stuff," his editor had cautioned. "Only headline-worthy news."

"Do you realize how impossible it is to find an earthshaking story at a church?" C.H. had grumbled to his boss. "There's nothing newsy there. All that happens is preaching, collections, music, and things like that. I need a different assignment."

C.H. was tired of grumbling about his work and decided a little diversion would cool his angst. So he rented a canoe and vigorously rowed to the middle of the lake. That's where it happened.

He was clumsily fussing with his fishing gear when he tried to stand up in the small craft. That was a big mistake. The canoe became badly unbalanced, and his overcorrection dumped him into the cold water. His panic attempt to swim to shore proved futile, and he was finally dragged ashore by others.

He could still smell the lake water in his nostrils, and his frantic flailing and utter exhaustion were stabbed deep into his consciousness. He expected to be in great pain. But as he looked about, C.H. felt a peaceful calm. An ethereal spirit wafted through him. He had a sense of being on a higher plane. "I think I've been raptured."

Trying to reconcile his situation, C.H. looked out across the lake, hoping to locate the capsized canoe. "I'll never rent another boat, that's for sure," he mumbled.

As he searched for the overturned canoe, he saw a flashing silver light reflecting on the water. It looked…unnatural. "Is that a UFO?" The light moved toward him.

"What the heck?" he muttered.

As the strange light continued to move in his direction, his journalistic instincts kicked in. "Maybe this is the big story I've been looking for," he said, squinting as the light advanced toward him.

"What the heck?" he repeated, intent on the light.

The light came closer, and a baritone voice came from it. It said, "This way."

C.H. sensed a gravity-like force tug at him. "Just a minute. Hold on." But as he spoke, he found himself moving, like a gossamer shadow, away from the lake and to a place of light unlike any he had ever seen.

The voice came again from the flashing light. "The Lord God has sent me to speak to you because you have searched for Him and not found Him."

The light became less blinding. C.H. blinked hard. Suddenly, right before him stood a radiant angel. He was dazzling white and appeared translucent.

"I know I'm dead because I'm looking at a spirit creature," he whispered.

The angel said, "Perhaps you have forgotten. You prayed for a story about Jesus."

"I—I did?" C.H. stuttered.

"Yes. But your search has been in vain because your heart is not right. You do not have eyes to see nor ears to hear, yet you have been close to the greatest story ever told."

"The greatest story ever told?" The words punched C.H.'s eager ears. He was ready to put on his reporter's gloves and go to work.

But a feeling of caution came to him like a small warning bell in his ear. He felt his courage recoil a bit. He sensed that he was hearing the voice of authority. He needed to watch his step. This was no time for his usual irreverent, brassy journalism to show itself.

I won't get in his face, C.H. thought. *But I have to hear this story.*
With some trepidation he said, "Tell me about the greatest story."

"Because you have searched in vain, the Lord God has sent me to help you find the story of the Bread of Heaven…if you wish to find it."

"Bread of Heaven?" C.H. snorted. Didn't sound like headline news to him.

"Because you are created in God's image, you are a free moral agent. The Lord God would like for you to solicit His wisdom. However, He is giving you a choice. You may choose to find the story of the Bread of Heaven, or you may choose to hear the story of the Lord's return."

"The Lord's return? Are you saying I could learn the exact day and time Jesus will come back?"

"If you choose that story, you will discover precisely when Jesus will come back to earth to claim His own."

C.H. gave a long, low whistle. "Now, that's a headline."

"If you choose the right story, you may return to your body, and to your newspaper, and write the story. If you choose the wrong one, then you must write the story in Paradise."

In a slow and cautious voice, C.H. said, "May I ask a question?"

"What is it?" asked the angel.

"Could you just verify one thing? Is He really coming back? I mean, I am a Christian, you know, but…"

"Yes," said the angel. "It's true."

C.H. grinned. "What a great lead. I can see the headlines now."

"The world would ignore such a story," said the angel. "But the choice is yours."

"How about I work on both of them?"

"You must choose only one."

C.H. took a deep breath. "OK. Then I choose the story of Jesus' return. My editor is gonna love it!"

"But your editor will never hear the story," said the angel.

"What do you mean?" C.H. felt himself moving away from the angel. "Wait a minute!" he yelled. "What's going on?"

"You are headed to eternity," said the angel. "Or have you changed your mind?"

"Hold on a minute, OK?" C.H. stopped moving. "Let me think. If I go to that place to write the story of Jesus' return, does that mean I'm going to be dead…forever?"

"That is correct," said the angel. "You have already been declared clinically dead. And you will remain that way unless you can save your life by finding the Bread of Heaven."

A sharp pain of reality struck C.H. in the stomach.

The angel continued. "You have displeased the Most High because you have chosen folly. The Lord God will not help you unless you are willing to choose wisdom."

The extreme urgency of his situation came into focus. C.H. wanted to cry. Thoughts flashed through his head with the speed of light. I've got to get published. But I don't want to die.

Finally, he said, "OK. I choose the other story."

"Are you sure?" asked the angel. "Will you commit to search for the Bread of Heaven?"

"Yes, yes."

"Perhaps you do not grasp your precarious situation," said the angel. "There is too much to gain to risk any chance of losing. Would you like me to explain some things about death and what follows?"

"No, please don't. My stress is already up to here," said C.H., saluting his chin. "I want the bread. Really."

"Very well," said the angel. "I will help you in your search, but first I have a question. Do you read the holy Scriptures?"

"Sure," said C.H., even though he almost never read the Bible.

"Then you know what the Lord God said to Hosea, son of Beeri."

"Huh?"

"He said, 'When Israel was a child, I loved him, and out of Egypt I called my son.'" Hosea 11:1 NIV

"That was when Joseph and Mary were hiding from ol' Herod, who wanted to kill baby Jesus, right?"

"Yes and no," said the angel. "When you learn the secret from long ages past, which has been hidden in Egypt, you will learn that it was the nation of Israel that was in Egypt as a child, and you will know that the Lord's words portend a larger meaning than simply fleeing from Herod."

"Whatever you say," said C.H. "So, I'm ready to hustle. Let's find that bread."

"All right," said the angel. "We will begin the search for the Bread of Heaven."

"Can we make it snappy? I am drowning, you know."

"Do not worry. A thousand years is like a day to the Lord, and all things are possible with God."

"Hey, you got a name?" asked C.H. as he tried to grasp the reality of eternity.

"The Lord God has sent me to help you. Call me Helper. Now, we do have some ground rules."

"Ground rules?" asked C.H.

"While I am with you, you will be as I am. You will be able to see but not be seen. You will be able to hear but not be heard. But when I leave you, you must continue your search for the Bread of Heaven as a man, and live as a man."

The angel wanted C.H. to understand more than just ground rules. He wanted him to lift his vision to see the majesty and glory of the Most High. He said, "Through the ages the Creator has spoken to the wise and the faithful through the language of symbolism. You must learn to read God's signs, for they are great and amazing. His signs and wonders are His signature on the canvas of creation."

"Oh, I know where you're going with this," said C.H. "I've heard about the secret code in the Bible."

"All that you have heard about a secret code in the Bible is false," said the angel. "But there is a higher language that opens vistas of learning for the wise. God is the Designer. His graphics reveal His design, and

His real-life pictures reveal His truth. Words can be disputed, but His signs are indisputable."

"Got it," said C.H. "Pictures trump words. But…"

"But what?" asked the angel.

"Well, I'm sure you just misspoke."

Helper stared at C.H., waiting for an explanation.

"You said, 'When the nation of Israel was a child.' You meant Jacob, right? The man who was later given the name Israel."

"No, I meant nation," said the angel. "Israel, the man, was never in Egypt as a child. He was a grandfather when his name was changed to Israel, and he was in Penial at that time. The word of the Lord that came to Hosea, son of Beeri, does not refer to the man Israel. The only Israel that was in Egypt as a child was the nation of Israel."

"Of course," he said, pulling at his chin and trying to understand.

"Are you ready to start your search for the Bread of Heaven?"

"You bet. Let's go."

"All right, then, follow me." The moment the angel spoke, time and distance fled away.

To Canaan

"Follow me," said the angel.

C.H. and the angel moved at the speed of thought, and immediately before them appeared the ancient land of Canaan.

"Hey, look at that," said C.H., pointing. "A tent city. What town is that?"

"What you see is the home of one family," said the angel.

"Thirty tents for one family?" he said. "Wow! Must be a heck of a family."

Besides tents, C.H. saw donkeys, camels, sheep, and cattle. He also saw people tending the animals and doing other chores. Some women were shearing sheep. He saw provender bins for crop storage and a wagon yard. Smoke plumes rose from various outside ovens and cookeries.

"I will show you Canaan, and I will show you Egypt," said the angel, "for God's signs have been woven into events in these two places. The story reveals a secret that has been hidden through the generations. Learn the story, and it will guide you as you search for the Bread of Heaven. Wisdom declares that God's signs are wonderful."

"W–where…" stuttered C.H.

"This way," said the angel. "Follow me."

Wide eyed and apprehensive, C.H. followed the angel. They soon came upon some men having a discussion.

"Those men are all Jacob's sons," said the angel. "It is harvest time in Canaan, and these brothers have been working in the fields to bring in the crops."

One of the sons, a teenager, was eagerly talking to his brothers. The boy wore a long coat of many colors.

"What do you see?" asked the angel.

"I see a kid in a gaudy coat. Looks like he's being a real nuisance. He's wearing all the colors of the rainbow. He could be a fan of every team in the world. Except I don't see any pinstripes."

"What else do you see?" asked the angel.

"A bunch of grown men, the teenager, and a child. If I understood you correctly, I'm looking at Jacob's sons."

"True," said the angel. "This is the most significant family in all of history. This is the nation of Israel in its infancy."

As C.H. stared at the brothers, they gained a new dimension of significance in his mind. "Which of Jacob's sons is that?" he asked, pointing to the young man in the coat.

"That is Joseph," the angel said. "Son of Jacob, the son of Isaac, the son of Abraham."

"You're kidding, right?" C.H. said, caught completely off guard. "You mean that dumb kid is Jacob's favorite? The shepherd boy from the Bible who became governor of Egypt?"

"That is correct," replied the angel. "Are you familiar with the story?"

"Hey, I've read it a dozen times," said C.H. Exaggeration came naturally to him. "I've read the Bible, and I've been to Sunday school. How do you think I got the church assignment?" C.H. looked at the young man again. "But if that kid is Joseph, then…then we're back in time."

"Yes," said the angel. "From your perspective. We are now thirty-nine generations prior to the birth of God's Son."

C.H. took a deep breath. "Wow! B.C., that's like a million years ago." Quickly, he tried to reconstruct his knowledge of Jacob's family.

The angel read his mind. "Twelve," he said. "Twelve sons and one daughter. Joseph is the eleventh, and the child, Benjamin, the twelfth. Both are sons of Rachel."

For an instant C.H. thought he heard weeping, but then it was gone. He looked about at the surroundings.

"This is where Joseph grew up, huh?" he said, holding his arms out wide to encompass the many tents of the extended family.

"He has lived here since he was six years old. Now, he is seventeen."

Joseph was still talking to his brothers, but C.H. couldn't make out the words.

"We will move closer," said the angel. "It is important that you hear what he is saying, because he is telling his brothers about a dream God sent him. It greatly exceeded any common dream. He is hoping his brothers will help him understand what great things the dream might portend."

As they came closer, C.H. pressed his finger to his lips in a sleuth manner, suggesting to the angel that they be quiet.

"They can neither see us nor hear us," said the angel.

"Oh, yeah. I forgot."

C.H. listened carefully as Joseph told his brothers about his dream. He could tell from the looks on the brothers' faces, and from their body language, that the story was not being well received.

"Please hear this dream that I dreamed," said Joseph. "We were binding sheaves of grain out in the field when suddenly my sheaf rose and stood upright, while your sheaves gathered around mine and bowed down to it." Genesis 37:7 NIV

Like a bomb exploding, the brothers responded with an outburst of anger.

"What's their problem?" asked C.H., backing away. "Why are they so upset?"

"Jealousy. It has been building for years. They know how much their father loves Joseph. He is Rachel's son. He is virtuous and beautiful of body, with a keen and prudent mind. They know that their father, Jacob, loves him very much…more than he loves them."

One of the enraged brothers kicked up a cloud of dust. They all snorted their resentment and threw their arms in the air.

C.H. quickly hid behind the angel. "We've got trouble, right here in Tent City."

The angel turned and looked at C.H. as if to say, "Why are you hiding?"

"OK." He shrugged apologetically. "I remember the ground rules. While I'm with you, they can't see me or hear me. When I'm not with you, I must live as a man. Hey, you're not going to leave me, are you?"

"Not yet."

"Good." He breathed a sigh of relief. "These ancients are a tough generation. Look at those guys! They're hard as rocks, and they're not happy. That kid had better watch it or they'll have him for lunch."

"Behold, you are looking at one of God's amazing signs," said the angel. "Observe carefully, because God's signs are great. To understand the language of God, you must learn to read His signs."

"I don't see any signs," said C.H.

"Much symbolism began with this family. Maybe you should start by observing the father-son relationship between Jacob and Joseph. Their love was unique. They were two men, but one spirit. View this story as living prophecy that foretells the story of Jesus. Every detail is significant. The stories of Joseph and Jesus are parallel stories."

"I don't get it," said C.H. "What do you mean?"

"The story of Joseph foreshadows the story of Jesus, and it clarifies much theology. One story walks in the symbolic footsteps of the other. A newspaperman like yourself might call the story of Joseph an early edition of the story of Jesus." The angel smiled, then continued. "The story of Joseph also reveals the secret of eternal life. Those who receive the Bread of Heaven live forever."

"So you're saying this story has a connection to the bread?" C.H. asked.

"Yes. And this is the story you chose to write. Now, open your eyes to symbolism and behold God's signs and wonders."

C.H. pulled at his chin, which was his habit when in deep thought. "Can we say that the stories of Joseph and Jesus are congruent?"

"Indeed," said the angel. "There are many points of congruency in the two stories. One is more about physical matters, and the other is mostly about spiritual matters. Yet there are parts of both stories that are physical and parts of both that are spiritual."

"I've read the story of Joseph. But now that I've actually seen him and heard him speak, I can tell you that kid is just a silly dreamer, and not too smart."

The angel shook his head. "Remember, your life is in the balance. You need to put a little slack in your frustration and understand your predicament. If you search with diligence, you will find the Bread of Heaven and save your life."

A battle between faith and skepticism tore at C.H.'s soul.

"Keep this in mind," the angel said. "Physical matters on earth may symbolize spiritual matters in high places."

"Well," said C.H., "if that kid becomes governor of Egypt, I'll…" He didn't finish his thought.

"All things are possible with God. But see for yourself if Joseph becomes governor."

"Yeah, I want to see that."

"First, you need to hear another dream. Joseph had parallel dreams, and it is crucial that you hear the second one."

"You mean the kid is going to risk his life again?"

It was another day in Canaan, and C.H. and the angel came close to listen as Joseph told his brothers about his second dream.

"I hope the kid is a little smarter this time," C.H. said.

"Listen carefully," the angel advised, "because you are about to hear the most profound dream in all of history."

C.H. listened, hushed and breathless.

"Listen. Please hear my other dream," Joseph said. "I had another dream, and this time the sun and moon and eleven stars were bowing down to me." Genesis 37:9 NIV

The brothers stood frozen in disbelief that Joseph would tell such an absurd dream.

Jacob shifted his posture, obviously astounded by Joseph's dream. He also looked confused and uncomfortable.

"Wow," C.H. said. "That's over the top. The sun and the moon? The kid is dumber than I thought. He can't get away with that. They'll kill him."

"Peace," said the angel. "The Lord God wanted you to hear the two dreams because they prophesy great things. This opens a vista into your search for the Bread of Heaven."

"How so?" C.H. asked.

"These dreams concern two men who are loved by their fathers; one is the perfect model, while the other is the perfect Man. The two men lived thirty-nine generations apart. There were two dreams, two men, two lives, two tragedies, two victories, with many points of congruency."

"Are you saying Joseph had parallel dreams, and the dreams symbolize parallel stories?" asked C.H.

"Yes. The first dream concerned Joseph, and it came true when his brothers traveled to Egypt for grain and bowed down before him. The second dream was about Jesus. You see, Joseph, the model, dreamt the dream of the one he modeled. The second dream came true when Jesus was glorified and God gave Him all power in heaven and on earth. The sun, the moon, and the stars all bowed down to Him. Both dreams were prophetic, and both dreams came true."

"That all sounds pretty lofty," said C.H. "But I have a problem. I'm not too impressed with that kid. So far he has acted pretty dumb. What was he trying to do, get himself killed?"

"You may stop your search anytime," said the angel.

"Sure, and then I'll be dead, right?"

"That's right," said the angel.

C.H. felt deep fear and frustration. "No way. I'm not quitting. I've got to find the bread. Besides, no good reporter quits in the middle of a story." He turned his eyes toward heaven and thought about his life-and-death predicament. "Guess I'm between a rock and a hard place."

"Every man is between a rock and a hard place," said the angel. "Follow me."

C.H. followed the angel to a different time and place. There he saw a young man climbing a hill. At the top of the hill, he stopped and looked around.

"There's Joseph again," said the angel. "His father, Jacob, has sent him to find his brothers and their herds. And as you have well stated, his life is in danger."

Joseph shielded his eyes as he searched the horizon, looking for his brothers. They were nowhere in sight.

"The harvest is over," said the angel, "and Jacob has sent his sons with their herds to Shechem to find pasture."

"Herds? I don't see any herds," said C.H.

"Nor does Joseph," replied the angel. "The brothers have disobeyed their father and moved the herds away from Shechem."

C.H. watched Joseph continue to search. "Beloved Son Searches for Lost Brothers," said C.H., thinking like a journalist. "Is that parallel to something?"

With his large family, Jacob had spread his tents in Hebron, and the hearty clan had done well for the past eleven years. Jacob was richer than his neighbors, and he and his family, with his many sons and one daughter, were well respected. He was a happy man, and he felt very blessed. The inhabitants of the country looked upon him and his family with envy and admiration. They saw each member of the family as strong in mind and body, capable of enduring great toil, and shrewd in understanding.

On this occasion Jacob had sent his seventeen-year-old son, Joseph, with a message for his older brothers. He wanted his son to bring back a report from the herdsmen. The teenager would have to walk fifty miles north from Hebron, over the mountains, and past Jerusalem. The round-trip journey would be a one-hundred-mile trek on foot.

Now, Jacob was apprehensive about his beloved son taking the long journey. He knew the dangers, and he feared for Joseph's safety. But he knew Joseph could be trusted to obey his father's will.

However, as Joseph approached Shechem, his eyes found nothing but an empty horizon. Not only had the brothers moved, they had done another sinister thing. In their seething anger and jealousy against Joseph, they had ratified an evil agreement amongst themselves to kill him.

"I smell trouble," said C.H.

"Here is a good place to start your search for points of congruency," said the angel. "The story of Joseph prophesies about the Bread of Heaven. God's signs are great, and they will bring light to your path. You can learn about Jesus by watching Joseph."

"What can I learn from a dumb kid who can't even find his family?" asked the journalist.

"Have faith. The pearl of great price hides behind faith. Consider this a treasure hunt, for a treasure that is worth more than the whole world. Every point of congruency is a clue leading to the mother lode of all treasure. For example, here you find Joseph faithfully doing the will of his father, who loved him in a special way. He is searching for his jealous brothers, who hate him. Now, do you see how that prophesies about Jesus?"

"Not really. I mean, Joseph wasn't too smart. And his brothers really hated him."

"That's your first point of congruency," said the angel. "Those who wanted to kill Joseph symbolize those who wanted to kill Jesus."

C.H. perked up. "Oh, I get it. So that's what you mean by points… symbolism."

"Yes," said the angel. "You will now live here as a man and search for points of congruency. Remember the ground rules. You are a journalist searching for a story. But more than that, you are on a treasure hunt, searching for life."

"You're making me nervous," said a confused C.H. "You sound like you're about to leave."

"I must leave you for a while, but the Lord God will help you search for the Bread of Heaven."

C.H.'s mouth dropped open, and he felt pain in his gut.

"When you have covered the events of Canaan, I will show you Egypt," said the angel. "God's signs are great, and His language is truth. His cast is many, and His script will become Scripture."

"Wait a blessed minute," he cried. "This is scary."

"Be not afraid. Learn to pray, and trust the Lord. As long as you seek Him and search for the Bread of Heaven, He will never leave you nor forsake you."

In an instant C.H. lost his out-of-body feeling. The sense of being at a higher level left him, and he felt the gritty sensation of his flesh-and-bone body standing on the dusty ground of Canaan.

His slightly out-of-shape body felt familiar, and he flexed his arms, shook his legs, and turned his head back and forth to reorient himself. He felt his clothing and discovered he was dressed like an ancient Hebrew citizen. "Are you really about to leave me?" he asked.

The angel spoke softly. "It is time for me to leave and let you begin your search."

"I've been divorced by two wives and fired from three newspapers," said C.H., "but I've never been dumped this fast."

"Be of good cheer," urged the angel. "Be open minded, and expect surprises. Be alert, and watch for that which symbolizes the Bread of Heaven."

"You mean I'm supposed to live here in these weird ancient times and try to follow that kid around?" C.H. stamped his sandaled foot. "We'll both be killed. I might as well drown."

"If you do not find the Bread of Heaven, you are already dead. But if you find the Bread of Heaven, you will always be alive and no one can kill you."

C.H. held his hands out wide. "How am I supposed to live? What do I eat? How do I get around? What do I do here? This ain't gonna work."

"You may quit if you wish. Or you can pray. Pray to the Lord God, and He will help you."

As C.H. stood there in the empty pasture at Shechem, peering at a kid searching for his brothers, he heard someone yell out greetings to Joseph. The stranger approached and spoke to Joseph. He said he had overheard Jacob's sons say they were going to Dothan. The stranger pointed toward the distant horizon.

C.H. gave a dismissive wave. "I still don't see governor material. I can tell you right now, it ain't going to happen." He jerked his head toward where the angel had last stood. But Helper had disappeared. "Guess I'm talking to myself."

C.H. remembered the story of Jacob's love for Joseph, which had grown strong through grief. Jacob had many children, and he loved them all. But Joseph was special because he was Rachel's firstborn. From the day he first laid eyes on her, Rachel was the true love of his heart, and she had died giving birth to her second son, Benjamin.

"Yeah," C.H. mumbled to himself, "I guess Rachel died so Benjamin could live. Maybe that's another point of congruency: somebody dying so that somebody else can live."

The weeping sound came to C.H.'s ears again. He listened carefully. "It's a woman." The sound went away as quickly as it came. C.H.

scratched his head in wonderment, then quickly returned his thoughts to Benjamin.

"I'm glad Benjamin isn't part of that angry bunch," C.H. said, still keeping an eye on Joseph. "Now, there's a love triangle…sorta. Jacob, Joseph, and little Ben. They all love one another. Maybe baby brother symbolizes somebody who loves Jesus."

Jacob's family had come into being through some amazing struggles. Jacob's father-in-law, Laban, tricked him and forced him to marry Leah, Rachel's older sister. Yet Jacob's love for Rachel was strong, and he worked many years for the hard-dealing Laban to earn the right to marry his true love.

It was the start of the world's most significant family. Jacob produced children with four women: first Leah, then Leah's handmaiden, then Rachel's handmaiden. Finally, in response to her heartfelt prayers, Rachel was able to give Jacob children. Joseph was her firstborn.

C.H.'s musings stopped abruptly when he realized that Joseph had taken off and was heading down the hill at a fast pace. Though he'd already walked a long distance, Joseph set out with long, swift strides to cover another fifteen miles to Dothan.

The frightened, sputtering journalist stumbled after him. *When I asked my editor for a new assignment, I sure didn't mean something like this,* he thought. *How am I supposed to get a story following this sheepherder kid?*

C.H. soon started huffing and puffing as he tried to keep pace with the youngster. "Wait up," he muttered. "I'll never keep up with that kid. He could win a marathon."

C.H. had to stop and take a breather.

"That kid is certainly not hiding. My gosh, you can see his multicolored coat for a hundred miles." He gasped. "I suppose all those colors probably symbolize something."

C.H. flopped down on a grassy incline and gave a disgusted good-bye wave to Joseph. "Man, he moves fast. I guess he's in a hurry to get killed." He watched Joseph stride across the countryside until he disappeared out of sight.

C.H. sat there for several minutes, staring across the landscape. When his stomach started rumbling, he muttered to the empty horizon, "I'll have a hamburger, please. With plenty of mustard and onion. And throw in some fries and a cup of coffee too. Oh, baby, would that taste good right now! You'd think a dead man wouldn't need to eat."

He felt the evening air getting colder. "How am I gonna get out of this mess? I'm dead, and I'm miles from anywhere in a place that hasn't existed for about a million years."

He felt tears stinging his eyes and brushed them away. "I guess I'm gonna die in my sins after all." He kicked the ground in disgust. "Why did God save me from drowning just to let me die here?"

C.H. lay on the ground and started kicking and screaming the way he had when he was four years old. "Maybe I should never have been born."

He recalled the angel's words. "Before he dumped me, Helper said I should pray to the Lord God, and He would help me. I wonder…Maybe I'll give it a try."

C.H. stood. "Betcha old Abraham would raise his arms toward heaven." He stretched his arms to full length. "OK, here goes. God, this is C.H. Roland, the journalist. You remember, I talked to you about a story? Well, I drowned. And now I'm in this old Bible place with Joseph."

He figured God probably knew all that. But it helped him to say it out loud, so he continued. "I'm sure you know your angel, the one called Helper? Well, he said—"

Instantly, the angel appeared in front of him. Startled, C.H. stumbled and fell on his backside. "Helper!" he cried. "Man, that was quick."

"What can the Lord God do for you?" asked the angel.

"For starters," he said, standing and dusting himself off, "how about explaining to me what it is I'm supposed to be looking for in this barren place? I can't keep up with that kid. He's like a greyhound! So just tell me, am I looking for some kind of manna or what?"

"Manna is not the Bread of Heaven," said the angel. "Have you not read the Scripture that speaks of the Bread of Heaven?"

C.H. gave the angel a blank look.

The angel said, "This is the bread that came down from heaven. Your forefathers ate manna and died, but he who feeds on this bread will live forever." John 6:58 NIV

"Oh, sure, I knew that," C.H. bluffed.

The angel was silent. It was a knowing silence, and C.H. realized he was not fooling anyone.

"I don't think following Joseph through Canaan is going to help me find what I'm looking for," he shot back defensively. "If you want my opinion, I think he's going to get killed."

"If you know this story, then you know that Joseph is not going to be killed," said the angel.

"Hey, I saw his brothers. They're plenty jealous. Who knows? Maybe the story got mixed up."

"But Joseph is going to be taken to Egypt, where he will become governor," said the angel.

"That dumb kid is in big trouble here. I'll give odds it don't happen."

"Your frustration is fighting your faith," said the angel.

"Yeah, whatever." C.H. shrugged. Then a thought struck him. "Hey, why can't I wait for him in Egypt, where there's food and shelter?"

The angel said, "Very well, it is your choice. The Lord God grants your wish. You may search for the secret of ages past in Egypt. There you will discover how the stories of Joseph and Jesus are parallel stories."

C.H. heaved a sigh of relief.

"The story of Jesus cast a shadow back in time," continued the angel. "The shadow came first, before that which cast it."

"Interesting," mused C.H.

"You remember what the Lord God said to Hosea, son of Beeri. When God said He would call His Son out of Egypt, He meant that He would cause that shadow to materialize into that which cast it."

"I think I'm beginning to get the picture."

"You will see for yourself how the Egyptians were saved from starvation by the bread of Egypt, and you will learn what symbolizes the Bread of Heaven. You can lift the eyes of your understanding about Joseph's dreams."

"All right, then, let's go to Egypt."

"If you go to Egypt now, you will miss the part of the story that started in Canaan. But you may do as you wish."

"Don't worry about my missing part of the story. I'm a good journalist," bragged C.H. "I can fill in the blanks."

Joseph in Canaan

Trouble brewed ahead as Joseph hustled across the countryside, but there was no suspicion or fear in his heart. He trekked for hours toward Dothan. Like a lamb to the slaughter, he walked urgently, with long, swift strides and an undaunted spirit, willing to do his father's bidding.

His brothers' angry actions should have warned him. He should have been alerted when Levi, upon hearing his dream, said, "Do you intend to reign over us?" But Joseph's brotherly love left no room for animosity, and he did not cower, nor did he let his faith waver.

Extreme jealously raged in the brothers' hearts. Their minds were bent on evil when they looked across the countryside and saw the sun glistening off Joseph's coat of many colors.

"Look!" said one. "That dreamer is coming. Let's kill him."

Another said, "We can throw his dead body into one of these pits and say that a wild animal devoured him. That will end his dreams."

But Reuben, the eldest, tried to appease his brothers and protect Joseph from harm. "Let's not shed any blood. We could throw him into a cistern in this deserted place, but don't hurt him." Reuben said this because he planned to rescue Joseph and take him back to his father.

When Joseph came near and gave a cheerful greeting, his brothers, overcome with hatred, grabbed him and held him in a fast grip. They stripped him, took his robe of many colors, and threw him into a dry cistern filled with scorpions and snakes.

Reuben left to take his turn at tending the flocks. The other brothers walked a bow-shot distance away from the cistern to get away from the sound of Joseph's weeping and pleading. They found a place to sit, eat, and talk. As they ate their bread, they further debated killing their younger brother.

One brother pointed toward something in the distance. "Look," he said. "There on the road, coming from Gilead."

They all stood and looked at a barely visible caravan coming toward them. "Sons of Ishmael," said one.

The Ishmaelites were apparently on their way to Egypt, their camels loaded with spices, balm, and myrrh.

"What will we gain if we kill our brother and cover up his blood?" Judah said to his brothers. "I say we sell him to those Ishmaelites."

The proposal pleased the other brothers.

While the brothers waited for the Ishmaelites, who were still a long distance away, seven Midianite merchants came from another direction, searching for water. They saw vultures circling above a pit and rushed over to see what was in it. As they approached the pit, they heard Joseph weeping and pleading for his brothers to save him.

The men looked into the pit and were surprised to see a tearful youth who looked to be quite healthy in mind and body.

"Who are you?" one asked. "And how did you get into this pit?"

The men lifted Joseph from the pit, thinking they had found a valuable prize. They took him captive and proceeded on their way, which took them near the place where Joseph's brothers were eating their bread.

When the sons of Jacob saw that the Midianites had taken Joseph, they were outraged. "What are you doing with our servant?" one yelled. "Do you think you can steal him from the pit where we put him?

He rebelled against us, and we put him in the pit for punishment. You will do well to give him back immediately."

"Is this fine young man really your servant?" one of the Midianites asked. "He is more comely than you. Perhaps you are all his servants, and you are speaking falsely to us. We will not listen to your lies. We found the youth in a pit in the wilderness, and we are keeping him."

The brothers were greatly provoked. All except Simeon rose to their feet and drew their swords. "Give us our servant now, or you will all die by the edge of the sword," one of them warned.

The indignant merchants became furious at the threats and accusations. Their anger flared, and they drew their swords to fight the brothers.

As they stood facing one another, with swords drawn, Simeon rose from his sitting position. His fury made him an awesome sight as he drew his sword. From deep within his belly, his anger erupted into a battle shout that could be heard for a great distance. The Midianites felt the ground shake under their feet, and they were frozen in fear.

Simeon pointed his sword at the merchants. Peering through squinted eyes and speaking slowly in a low voice, he said, "I am Simeon, the son of Jacob the Hebrew."

After a slight pause Simeon thrust his sword toward the sky and shouted, "God powers my sword. My brother Levi and I slew all the males in the city of Shechem. We destroyed the cities of the Amorites. Even if all your brethren from Midian and all the kings of Canaan were here to help you, you could not win a fight against me."

Simeon stepped toward the Midianites. "Shall I give your flesh to the birds of the air and the beasts of the earth? Or do you wish to return the youth you have stolen?"

The merchants' will to fight wilted in an instant. They sheathed their swords in a display of surrender. "You put your rebellious slave in the pit," one said. "Slave owners must not tolerate disobedience. You must have been justified to put him in there."

When it appeared to the Midianites that their talk had allayed Simeon's sword, they thought it safe to talk business. "But what will you do with him now? He will surely misbehave again. If you would consider selling him to us, we would pay your full price."

All but Reuben, who was away tending the herd, felt it was the perfect solution to rid themselves of Joseph. So they sold him to the anxious merchants for twenty pieces of silver.

Then the guilty brothers, with their pieces of silver, devised another devious plot. They agreed to deceive their father. They would tell Jacob that Joseph had been killed by a wild beast. And they would give Jacob the cloak of many colors, which they would cover with an animal's blood.

The Midianites took Joseph and continued on their way toward Gilead. But they soon became remorseful over purchasing the handsome young Hebrew.

One said, "The small price we paid does not balance with truth. Those were hardy and powerful men, especially the fierce one. I think they stole the lad from an important family and sold him to us."

"Yes," said another. "He is a handsome, well-favored lad, and there is probably a large band of Hebrews already searching for him. Our lives are at stake. We must not be found with him as our captive."

"Look," said one of the merchants, pointing at the Ishmaelite caravan. "Let us sell this youth to those camel riders for the same small price we paid."

The Midianites sold Joseph to the Ishmaelites for twenty pieces of silver, then went on their way to Gilead.

The Ishmaelites set their newly purchased slave on a camel and continued their journey toward Egypt. They passed along the road of Ephrath by Bethlehem, where Rachel, his mother, was buried. Joseph wept bitterly.

Circumstances were driving Joseph's life toward what could be the world's most amazing adventure.

CHAPTER 4

C.H. Goes to Egypt

Follow me," said the angel.

At the speed of thought, C.H. found himself in Giza, a necropolis of Memphis, looking at an enormous burial tomb.

"That is called the Great Pyramid," said the angel. "It is the largest in all of Egypt. It is made up of 2,500,000 stones, and each stone weighs about two and a half tons. It took twenty years to build. When it was built, it was 481 feet high. It is more than a thousand years old at this point in time. It was built by the Egyptian pharaoh Khufu, for his burial place. He believed it would help him find a happy afterlife."

"Did it work?" asked C.H., though he already knew the answer to his question.

"No pyramid ever built, no matter how extravagant, achieved even a slight measure of immortality," replied the angel. "No man, from Adam to the last born on earth, will have a happy afterlife unless he receives the gift of the Bread of Heaven."

C.H. looked at the big pyramid. "Ol' Khufu and I are a lot alike. I'm fighting for my life just like he did. That's pretty frightening."

"You are seeking the free gift of eternal life," said the angel. "That is worth more than all the pyramids ever built."

C.H. had no idea that ancient Egyptian funerary would become a frightening experience in his search for the Bread of Heaven.

In the days of Joseph, Egypt was full of huge structures that were built for the glorification of kings and rulers. There was almost nothing Egyptian kings would not do to preserve their lives and glory.

All together there were about eighty pyramids in Egypt, and they were all built for the same purpose: to glorify proud Egyptians and to bring them a form of salvation.

The Sphinx is the image of a lion with the head of a man. It symbolizes a man with the power of a lion. Some believe its face depicts that of Pharaoh Khafre. It is a huge image, 240 feet long and 66 feet high, sculpted from one solid rock, with paws and legs added.

Early Egyptians believed in animal power. Because of this belief, some went so far as to wear animal disguises and fake tails, hoping that would bring them power.

C.H. looked at the big pyramid and said, "I don't go to funerals."

"Come with me," said the angel.

C.H. followed the angel to a place overlooking a site where dozens of men were working on a big structure that reached for the sky. "Wow, that's big," he said. "What is it?"

"That is an obelisk, reverently called Tejen by the Egyptians. We are now in a place called Karnak."

The angel explained to C.H. that the huge obelisk was more than ninety feet tall and weighed more than five hundred tons. The trunk was a monolithic, quadrangular, conical stone that had been quarried in Aswan and shaped into one smooth piece. The Pyramidon, the pointed, gold-plated top, was meant to keep negative forces away from the king.

C.H. noticed other observers near the place where he and the angel were watching. A small group of men in horse-drawn chariots, and a dozen spear bearers who ran along with the chariots, seemed to have a special interest in the work being done. One was dressed in royal Egyptian regalia, and his chariot had gold trimmings. His matched pair of horses were taller than the other horses.

C.H. remembered reading that in ancient Egypt, horses were rare, and only the privileged were fortunate to have them. The angel explained to him that horses had been introduced by Hyksos about three hundred years prior to Joseph's reign as governor. The relatively small Egyptian horses were between fifty and sixty inches in height. They were used to pull chariots, but rarely ridden.

"Who's that?" asked C.H.

"That is King Tutmosis III," replied the angel. "The Egyptians believe him to be a god."

"Are you saying that guy is Pharaoh?" asked C.H.

"Yes. He is here to watch the destruction of this obelisk."

C.H.'s mouth fell open. He noticed that the workers were digging a pit at the base of the huge obelisk. It was apparent that they were planning to dig the pit until the foundation was destroyed. It was also apparent that the diggers were in imminent danger.

Each digger in the pit had a rope tied about his waist. The opposite end of the rope was held by other men standing well out of harm's way. Those holding the ropes were ordered to watch for any movement of the giant stone and be ready to quickly assist the diggers out of the pit by tugging on the ropes. Other men stood watching; some were yelling instructions.

"Why are they doing that?" blurted the journalist, who thought this would make great headlines for the morning paper.

"Jealousy," answered the angel. "This obelisk was built for the glory of the former king, Hatshepsut, and the current king wants to destroy all memory of her."

"Her?" asked C.H., certain he'd heard wrong.

"Yes. Hatshepsut was a woman. She was Tutmosis III's stepmother. She wrested power from him after his father died, when he was yet a child. Now grown, he has reclaimed his birthright and seized supreme power in Egypt. He wants to destroy all memory of Hatshepsut."

"Did the Egyptians know their king was a woman?" asked C.H.

"Some did. But most did not. She wore a fake beard and acted like a man."

"Can anyone stop this?" asked C.H., cringing as the pit grew precariously large.

"Tutmosis III has absolute power in Egypt," replied the angel. "No one can stop him."

The king stepped down from his chariot and handed the horses' reigns to a member of his entourage. He strode forward a few steps and yelled to those who were in charge of the digging.

"What's he saying?" asked C.H.

"He wants more diggers in the pit," said the angel.

A half dozen fresh men scrambled into the pit, and others threw ropes to them. Those outside the pit yelled instructions, and the diggers bumped into one another in a frantic effort to dig faster.

Suddenly, a cry went up from those outside the pit, and those holding the ropes began to pull. The five-hundred-ton obelisk finally showed signs of movement. Slowly, it started to lean toward the pit.

As the ropes that were tied around the waists of the diggers were drawn tight, some men were yanked off their feet. Others were pulled toward men whose ropes were on the opposite side of the pit. The pullers worked against themselves, and the pit became a tangle of men and ropes. The men who had just entered the pit were still trying to get their ropes tied around themselves when their ropes were yanked out of their hands.

Like a dying giant, the stone tilted more. Then, as if all support on the pit side were suddenly gone, the obelisk came crashing to the ground. All the men made it out of the pit except two who had lost their ropes. They were crushed under five hundred tons of solid rock.

When the earthquake-like movement subsided and some of the dust settled, there was a moment of silence. Then a loud victory cry came from the king and his entourage. They drove away at breakneck speed. The king, with whip cracking, led the pack, and the spear bearers followed as fast as they could run.

C.H. felt sick to his stomach. "What kind of place is this? I thought Canaan was a dangerous place. But the first thing I see in Egypt is a murder."

"You must understand the people in this place. The Lord God has brought you here to search for the Bread of Heaven. You must learn about this man because you will live in Pharaoh's house and work for him, and he will test you severely."

"What?" C.H. snorted some choice expletives, threw his arms into the air, and stamped his feet. "You never said anything about—"

The angel stood motionless and silent for several minutes.

"I'm sorry," C.H. said quietly. "You're just trying to help me, and here I am yelling at you. And I apologize for my language."

The angel spoke quietly. "The Lord God knows about your language. He does not approve of it, nor of your drinking, your lying, your gambling, or your cheating. He knows you've been in jail. He knows that you are not a chaste man. Your heart needs renewing, and your faith is weak. The Most High is not helping you because of your righteousness."

"Then why is He helping me?" asked C.H.

"Because you have searched for Him. Anyone who diligently searches for God will find Him. You prayed for a story about Jesus. The Lord will grant your wish. But you must continue your search for the Bread of Heaven, and that search starts in this place. God's signs are in Egypt, and you need to learn to read God's signs."

"I want to read God's signs," C.H. said. "And I've got to find the bread. But why do I have to be here? God should have written this place off a long time ago."

"God will never forget Egypt, nor will He leave her. Are you not aware of His plan for this land of Egypt?"

The angel stood tall as if he were looking across all of Egypt. Holding one hand high, he said, "So the Lord will make himself known to the Egyptians, and in that day they will acknowledge the Lord. They will worship with sacrifices and grain offerings; they will make vows to the Lord and keep them." Isaiah 19:21 NIV

C.H. stood tall and followed the angel's gaze. Was Egypt really different?

The angel continued. "The Lord will strike Egypt with a plague: He will strike them and heal them. They will turn to the Lord, and He will respond to their pleas and heal them." Isaiah 19:22 NIV

"God must love this crazy place. He—"

The angel, not wanting to be interrupted, continued. "In that day there will be a highway from Egypt to Assyria. The Assyrians will go to Egypt and the Egyptians to Assyria. The Egyptians and Assyrians will worship together." Isaiah 19:23 NIV

"Someday these people are going to be Christians?" asked C.H. "That's a bunch of—"

Again, the angel refused to be interrupted. "In that day Israel will be the third, along with Egypt and Assyria, a blessing on the earth. The Lord Almighty will bless them, saying, 'Blessed be Egypt my people, Assyria my handiwork, and Israel my inheritance.'" Isaiah 19:24-25 NIV

"OK," C.H. said, "I confess, I've never heard that. But I still don't understand why God would bless this pagan place when the crazy king is so jealous of his dead mother that he goes around killing people."

"This Pharaoh has killed many men," said the angel. "You will do well to respect him as the king of Egypt. He is an instrument of God and has an important role in the story you are here to investigate."

"Oh," said C.H.

"Be at peace, and let God's signs come before you."

His mind racing to connect the dots, C.H. blurted out, "Is he the pharaoh who dreamed about the cows?"

"Yes," said the angel.

"Good grief! Joseph is in big trouble. That guy would not share his power with thunder and lightning. And Joseph is just a meek sheepherder kid."

C.H. thought about the teenager whose life was in danger in Canaan. He mumbled to himself, "If his brothers don't kill him, this guy will."

He looked at the angel and asked, "Does that guy think he's God?"

"Yes, he thinks he is God. So do all the Egyptians."

"Is he as glory hungry as the other guys who built all that big stuff?" asked C.H.

"Yes," said the angel. "Tutmosis III built four obelisks while he was king: two in Karnak and two in Heliopolis. But none remained. One of the two that were built in Karnak was moved to Rome and the other moved to Istanbul. One of the two built in Heliopolis is now in London and the other is in New York."

"You don't say," said C.H.

"The obelisk that was moved to New York is called Cleopatra's Needle, and most people who see it don't even know that it was Tutmosis III who built it. The slender, giant piece of granite took fifteen months to make its journey from Heliopolis to New York's Central Park in 1881."

"OK, tell me this: Did he kill what's-her-name, Hatshepsut?"

"She died in 1458 B.C., but only God knows how she died. Tutmosis III never lost a single battle, and historians call him the Napoleon of Egypt. He killed many men, but you should not accuse him of killing Hatshepsut."

C.H. was soon to learn much about Egypt's most unusual Pharaoh who wanted to destroy all memory of Hatshepsut.

CHAPTER 5

Joseph Goes to Egypt

"Levi," yelled Joseph. "Judah! Can you hear me? Please, I am your brother, your flesh and blood." His brothers ignored his pleading. Joseph's way of life had changed in one hour. The beloved, happy teenager who wore the regal, multicolored coat of honor was suddenly a slave.

He was sold for a pittance, and resold as worthless. He was beaten, yelled at, and mocked. He was carried to Egypt and sold yet a third and fourth time. Joseph's life was radically different.

The sons of Ishmael purchased Joseph for twenty shekels from the Midianites, and they brought him to Egypt. As they came near the borders of Egypt, they met four traders, the sons of Medan, who were just leaving Egypt on a trading trip.

The Ishmaelites were unhappy with the young slave, and they sold Joseph to the four traders for the price of twenty shekels.

The sons of Medan took one look at the handsome youth and began to envision large profits. Joseph resented them and feared how they looked at him. He heard them talk of an important man named Potiphar, who was seeking a good servant to stand before him and attend him. As captain of the guard, Potiphar was an officer of Pharaoh and high in the ranks, and the traders knew he could pay a large price for the right servant.

Joseph listened to the merchants talk of their plan to sell him to Potiphar, and he tried to explain that he was not a slave.

He sorely missed his father.

When Potiphar saw that Joseph was such a young, handsome specimen with high breeding, he was exceedingly pleased. "Tell me what you require for this youth."

The sons of Medan were eager for profit. One responded, "Four hundred pieces of silver."

"This comely youth is neither a slave nor the son of a slave," Potiphar said. "Perhaps he has been stolen. I will give you what you ask, but first you must bring proof that he is a slave and that you purchased him properly."

"Please hear me," said Joseph, desperate for someone to believe him. "I have been stolen."

But no one would listen. The four Medanim left him with Potiphar and hurried to find the Ishmaelites, then brought them back to testify regarding the purchase. So Joseph was sold for the fourth and final time to became a slave in the house of Potiphar.

Potiphar soon came to like the eighteen-year-old and was pleased with the addition to his household. He trusted Joseph, and soon after acquiring the handsome youth he placed full confidence in him and made him overseer of all household matters.

God blessed Joseph in all that he did. Thereby, Potiphar's house was blessed, and Joseph gained complete control of everything that came into the house or went out of the house.

The early days in Potiphar's house were days of learning and adapting. Joseph learned Egyptian culture, and he overcame the language barrier. He became proficient in all his duties.

Zelicah, Potiphar's wife, was attracted to Joseph from the first moment she saw him. As he grew into manhood, Joseph's physique became a well-shaped form of strength and beauty. He was, indeed, a handsome young man. Zelicah's heart melted under the gaze of his beautiful eyes and handsome face. She believed him to be the most comely man in all of Egypt. Her soul yearned for him, and she began enticing him.

One day she approached him and said, "Oh, how beautiful are your eyes. And how goodly is your appearance and your form. Truly, you will dazzle all of Egypt. I have seen all the slaves in this land, and there is not one so beautiful as you."

Joseph diverted his eyes to the ground. "My beauty and my glory belongs to my Creator. He who created me in my mother's womb created all mankind."

Zelicah was determined. Another day she interrupted his work and said, "It thrills me to hear your voice. Here, take this harp and play music, and let me hear you sing."

Joseph declined the harp and answered, "My words are beautiful and pleasing when I speak of my God and His glory."

His rejections did not cool Zelicah's desires, and she would not leave him alone. Another day she came to him and said, "I adore your hair, Joseph. Let me style it with this golden comb." She had brought a comb and some ointment, wanting to comb his hair and apply ointment to his body.

"How long will you do this?" asked Joseph as he hurried away. Over his shoulder he called back to her, "Leave me alone and go about your own affairs."

But Zelicah was persistent. She became more overt in her sexual advances. She went to great extremes to make herself enticing. She dressed immodestly and paraded before him, exposing herself to entice him.

Joseph became apprehensive and began planning his work to avoid Zelicah as much as possible. When he ignored her and refused to look at her, she said, "If you do not do as I wish and love me, I will punish you and put an iron yoke upon you."

But Joseph continued to resist all contact with her. This tore at Zelicah's heart. She threw herself into a grievous lovesickness. She fell on her bed and refused food and water. She made demands on other servants and screamed at them and punished them without cause.

Joseph was pleased when Zelicah became pregnant and gave birth to Potiphar's son. Maybe, he thought, this was the solution to his problem. He hoped she would be so absorbed with domestic matters, she would cease her flirtations with him. He became less suspicious, and stopped planning ways to avoid her.

Each year at the time of the inundation, when the Nile River rose above its banks, all the Egyptians celebrated. This annual event brought promise of a good harvest in the land. Everyone in Egypt went out with timbrels to a place of dancing and celebration.

Such was the case in Potiphar's house. Each year Joseph excused the entire household to join the happy throng and celebrate. But he remained home alone to attend the house.

One year Zelicah anticipated Joseph's plan to stay home alone. She claimed to be indisposed and remained in the house. She dressed herself in her best garments. She placed precious stones on her head and beautified herself with purifying liquids. She perfumed herself and the house with cassia and frankincense, and she spread myrrh and aloes about. Then she sat in the entrance of the house, where she knew Joseph would pass when he returned from the field.

Her passions boiled in the empty house as she kept a vigilant watch for sight of Joseph returning from the field. When she saw him coming, Potiphar's passion-ravished wife went to the gate to meet the young Hebrew.

Once before, Joseph's life had taken a sharp turn, and in one hour he was reduced from a favorite son to the level of a slave. This was to be another fateful day for the young man upon whom God had placed His signs and wonders. While Joseph was a healthy, normal young man, he was the model of the Savior of the world, and God had placed His signs upon a chaste model.

As Joseph entered the gate, Zelicah moved very close to him, reached out a caressing hand, touched his cheek, and said, "Come to bed with me."

Joseph quickly stepped around her and entered the house. He paused at the door and looked at Zelicah. "With me in charge," he told her, "my master does not concern himself with anything in the house; everything he owns he has entrusted to my care. No one is greater in this house than I am. My master has withheld nothing from me except you, because you are his wife. How then could I do such a wicked thing and sin against God?" Genesis 39:8,9 NIV

Zelicah pursued Joseph and grabbed him. Again she said, "Lie with me." She tugged at his coat. Joseph twisted and pulled free from her and ran outside, leaving her holding his coat.

Instant anger shot through the spurned and frustrated Zelicah. Suddenly, she wanted to punish Joseph.

When Potiphar and his household returned from the day of celebrating, she showed them Joseph's coat and accused him of attacking her.

C.H. in the King's Food Service

Ｃ.H. sat on a large stone, putting his elbow on his knee and his chin in his hand. He mumbled as he tried to make an assessment of his predicament.

"My drowned body is lying on the bank of Lynx Lake. I am in antiquity in a crazy land with an angel named Helper who tells me I have plenty of time and that I can return to the newspaper and write the story of the Bread of Heaven."

"What is your question, sir?" asked the angel.

"Why is God doing this?" asked C.H. as he stood and spread his arms wide.

"Have you forgotten your prayer?" asked the angel. "In your frustration as a journalist, you prayed for a story about Jesus. God is answering your prayer belatedly. Not all prayers are answered immediately."

"You mean like timed release?"

"In the meantime you chose to write about the Bread of Heaven, and now God is giving you the chance to write your story."

"Yeah, maybe. But I have a bigger problem."

"Correct," said the angel. "You say you are a Christian because you go to church. But the Most High knows your lack of faith. He is giving you the chance to pursue the story while you also find a way to save your life."

"OK, I see the problem here. I'm dead, and I don't have the bread. Forget the story."

"You want to forget the story?"

"It is a matter of priority. I need the bread. Why doesn't God just give me the Bread of Heaven right now, since that would save my life?"

"A dead person may not ask for the Bread of Heaven," said the angel. "It is too late for that. However, if you are able to find faith, and if you are able to learn the truth about the Bread of Heaven, the Lord God will let you return to your drowned body and write the story."

"That's fine, but I've got to have the bread."

"Once you are back in your body, you may then ask for the Bread of Heaven, and the Lord God will give it to you as a free gift."

"Sounds like a deal."

"Do you not know the Scripture? 'Which of you fathers, if your son asks for a fish, will give him a snake instead? Or if he asks for an egg, will give him a scorpion? If you then, though you are evil, know how to give good gifts to your children, how much more will your Father in heaven give the Holy Spirit to those who ask him!'" Luke 11:11-13 NIV

"I'll be asking, you can bet on that," said C.H. "And I will also get baptized when I get back in my ol' bod."

"Splendid," said the angel.

As C.H. and the angel spoke about the Bread of Heaven, some camels and riders approached and stopped nearby to look at the fallen obelisk. Camels were very unusual in Egypt in this time period, and the few that existed usually belonged to the king.

"Go speak to the man holding the last camel," said the angel. "He will hear your words in his own language, and you will hear his words in your language."

"That's a mean-looking guy."

The angel continued. "His name is Phygsis, and he is a powerful man in the service of the king. He and the men with him are eunuchs and slaves. Phygsis is in charge of the king's house, and the men with him are in the king's food service."

"What should I say?" asked C.H.

"The Lord will give you words," said the angel.

"This smells like trouble to me. I don't think I want to get mixed up with a bunch of castrated slaves."

"I thought you were anxious to know if Joseph becomes governor of Egypt. This is your chance to be an eyewitness."

"I already know his chances are zero," retorted C.H.

C.H. had much to learn about Egypt and Egyptian life.

Egypt is one of the oldest civilizations in the world and is located in northern Africa. It was made up of two kingdoms, the upper and the lower. The northern kingdom is where the longest river in the world, the Nile, flows into the Mediterranean Sea.

The Nile is over 4,200 miles long and it starts in the mountains of Africa. It flows for hundreds of miles through the great desert of the southern kingdom of Egypt and finally spreads out in a vast delta as it flows into the Mediterranean Sea. To the east of Egypt is the Red Sea.

Each summer, starting in June, there is a rainy season in the great mountainous watershed of the Nile that lasts for about three months. It is called the inundation, and it can raise the level of the water in the delta portion of the Nile by as much as thirty feet.

The river spreads out over a large area and deposits rich silt over many acres of Egyptian farmland. When the rainy season ends and the water recedes, Egyptian farmers set about to bring in a big harvest.

The Nile is the heart and soul of the Egyptian economy, and the city of Memphis has always been in the midst of the commercial activity. At one time Memphis was the capital, but in 2160 B.C. the capital was moved to Herakleopolis. Between the years of 2134 and 2000 B.C. the two kingdoms of Egypt were united and the capital was moved to Thebes.

The Egyptians believed the earth was flat and that the sky was held up by four poles so the air could flow between the earth and the sky.

They believed the Nile River was the center of the earth and that the earth was a circular area, beyond which lay the sea, filled with monster dragons.

C.H. had no idea how challenging Egyptian life could be. He looked back at Phygsis and repeated, "He looks mean."

Phygsis was slender and well built, and his upper body was bare. He wore a linen wrap from his waist to his ankles. His shaved head was covered with a close-fitting white cap that came down onto his forehead in the front, reached down his neck in the back, and was arched over each ear. He wore makeup on his face and black eyeliner on his lids.

C.H. had the strange feeling that Phygsis was expecting him. He took a few steps toward the man, then stopped and looked back. The angel was gone.

"Here," Phygsis called to him. "This is your camel. You will go with these men to Memphis."

C.H. mounted the animal with some difficulty, and the camel caravan made a half circle around Phygsis, who was staying behind. They waited for final instructions.

The eunuchs in the caravan were not just slaves, but special servants of the king. They carried royal power to claim anything they found that might please the king. Often they would purchase treasured items, but if the owner refused to sell, he was putting his life in danger.

They searched for special foods such as fruits, vegetables, fish, cheese, and poultry. They looked for fine wines too. And if they found gold, gems, or jewelry that might please the king, they claimed them for His Royal Highness.

C.H. was amazed that he could talk to the Egyptians and understand their language. He listened to every word of instruction that Phygsis gave to the departing eunuchs.

He quickly became fascinated with his new job and was able to put aside his life-and-death predicament. He especially liked the search for Egypt's best products. He became part of the team; he was in the king's food service.

They looked for musicians and entertainers to amuse the king. There was always a religious context to the music. The lyrics spoke of the god of music, which was Bes, and the goddess of music, Hathor. The king enjoyed both male and female voices and many kinds of musical instruments.

The king had others in his food service who did not ride camels. They sailed up and down the Nile in boats. There was an ongoing competition between the sailors and the camel riders to see which team could bring the best things to the king. One advantage the boat team had was that they could carry heavy loads and bring granite items from quarries up river.

One of the many Egyptian gods was named Hapy. Farmers worshipped Hapy, as they believed he brought the rain that made farming possible. He carried wheat, barley, dates, and flax. They envisioned him looking like a boat person.

There was a lot of commerce along the Nile. People bought, sold, and bartered cattle, coffee, wheat, furs, granite, and beer. Most boats were made of papyrus, but the king's boats were of cedar. They were much larger than the papyrus boats.

The average Egyptian had a life expectancy of about fifty years, and his diet consisted mainly of wheat bread and a heavy beer made from barley. Most farmers cooked their food outside or on the roof. They sat on the floor and slept on a mattress on the floor. If there were chairs or tables in the house, they were very low and not much different from sitting on the floor. Full-height chairs and tables were found only in wealthy, upscale houses.

Wherever the men in the king's food service went, they were welcomed into the homes and were given food and a place to sleep. C.H. and his food service companions stopped at several places, and he began to feel integrated. He enjoyed meeting the Egyptian families who welcomed him and the eunuchs into their homes.

The people knew the men were slaves of the king and that they were eunuchs. They presumed C.H. to be the same, and he had a strong feeling that he had better keep his personal matters secret.

One day they made a slow trek to multiple places along the Nile. As night approached C.H. and his companions directed their camels to a familiar house where they would seek food and shelter. When they arrived they learned that a family member had died. The house was full of mourners.

The eldest son was a hippopotamus hunter, and he had been killed in a hunt on the Nile River. The females in the extended family had smeared mud on their heads and faces, and they were wandering through the house and neighborhood, beating themselves and tearing at their clothes.

The master of the house suggested to the travelers that they go to a large house nearby, where a widow named Mahti lived by herself. He assured them that she would welcome them.

When they approached the widow, she appeared nervous and frightened. Nevertheless, she welcomed them and began to prepare some food. C.H. felt compassion for her and looked for some way to engage her in conversation. His journalistic instincts came forward and he began to gently interview her. After a few minutes Mahti relaxed and agreed to talk with C.H. privately while the others ate bread and drank barley beer. As time went by and the conversation continued, Mahti chatted more freely.

Mahti told C.H. that she once had a husband and a baby girl. She told of a time when she and her husband were shopping in a fish market when Hatshepsut, who was then Pharaoh, was traveling with her food service caravan, and she happened to come to the same fish market where Mahti was shopping.

Mahti was wearing her favorite jewelry, and Hatshepsut noticed it and wanted it.

The female king was wearing a fake beard and was dressed like a man. But she was still a woman, and she wanted the beautiful piece of jewelry. Mahti told how, even though she believed Pharaoh to be a god, she loved her jewelry and refused to sell it. Hatshepsut became angry and took her jewelry.

Mahti paused and looked at C.H. through tear-filled eyes, as if she were appealing to him. She shook with fear and pain as she whispered something she had kept locked in her heart for many years.

"Hatshepsut the king," she said, "took my jewelry and killed my husband and my baby girl."

Mahti began to sob violently. C.H. patted her on the shoulder, then walked out into the night air. *Maybe Tutmosis has a right to hate Hatshepsut*, he thought.

As C.H. stood outside thinking about the injustice that Mahti had received at the hands of Hatshepsut, he saw a lone rider approach Mahti's house. He got off his camel quickly and announced that he was searching for the men in the king's food service.

The men in the house came outside to discuss the matter. The rider explained that the king wanted them to return to the palace. He said that some of them were going to be reassigned to serve inside the palace. When asked why, he revealed that there had been a shakeup and that the king was reorganizing his staff. Many of the food service people inside the palace had been dismissed. Some had been put in prison, including the baker and the head wine server.

CHAPTER 7

John the Baptist

Any story about Jesus that does not include John the Baptist is not complete. The two men were spoken of in prophecy when God made known His plan for a Savior, and His great signs in Egypt did not fail to include John.

John's mission on earth was to go ahead of Jesus and announce him.

Joseph, in a parenthetical cameo, became the foreshadow of John the Baptist when he was living in Egypt. Potiphar's adulterous wife caused Joseph to go to prison, and Herod's adulterous wife caused John the Baptist to go to prison.

In the days of John the Baptist, Herod Antipas, the son of Herod the Great, married the daughter of Aretas, King of the Nabathaeans. On a trip to Rome, he fell in love with his niece Herodias, the wife of his half-brother, Philip, and he took her back to Galilee.

John, the fearless precursor of Jesus, rebuked Herod for his public adultery. The accusation caused Herodias to develop a bitter hatred for John. She persuaded Herod to arrest John and imprison him in the fortress of Machaerus, where he was later beheaded.

Thus ended the earthly life of the one about whom Jesus said, "I tell you, among those born of women there is no one greater than John; yet the one who is least in the kingdom of God is greater than he." Luke 7:28 NIV

Although John's body died, he did not die.

John and Jesus were cousins, and they are the only two men in the world who were born filled with the Holy Spirit. They both came into the world miraculously, and both were born in possession of eternal life.

John came into the world in the likeness of Elijah, and Jesus came into the world in the likeness of Melchizedek.

They were united by a single cause and by one Spirit, even though they were symbolically separated by ages, like morning and evening.

John was about six months older than his cousin. His was a miraculous birth by an aged mother with a barren womb. He symbolized the ending of the past age and the announcement of the new.

The Scripture says, "The Law and the Prophets were proclaimed until John. Since that time, the good news of the kingdom of God is being preached." Luke 16:16 NIV

Jesus' birth was even more spectacular than John's. He was born of a virgin mother and sired by the Holy Spirit. His birth symbolized the beginning of a new age. As the only begotten Son of God, he become the High Priest of a new covenant in the kingdom of God.

The Bible tells stories of great men of faith who were also sinners. While they were loved and blessed by God, they were far from perfect. Men like Abraham, Moses, David, Peter, and Paul lived and walked by faith, yet their sins are well known.

Abraham lied about his beautiful wife, Sarah, and handed her over to Pharaoh to save his own neck. Moses murdered an Egyptian. David was guilty of murder and adultery. Peter denied Christ. Paul killed Christians.

By contrast, Joseph was a seemingly perfect man. This is an interesting point of congruency because he modeled two men of miraculous birth: John the Baptist, the great precursor, and the Son of God, who was the perfect Man.

Joseph, the perfect model, was the predestined shadow of both John and Jesus. He modeled the only two men who were ever born filled with the Holy Spirit.

The years of faithful service that Joseph gave Potiphar were blessed by God. But Joseph was arrested and put in prison, even though he was not guilty of the crime for which he was accused.

While he was in prison, God was again with him and blessed him. God gave him favor in the sight of the warden, and once again Joseph was exalted. The warden put him in charge of the other prisoners, and he was given responsibility over all matters in prison.

CHAPTER 8

The Bread and the Wine

God's symbolism is amazing. He has used it as a higher language to speak to the wise and faithful throughout history and all around the world.

Jesus used symbolism to teach spiritual matters in high places. At the Last Supper He likened bread to His body and wine to His blood.

In the Bible, fire frequently symbolizes the Spirit. Sometimes called wind or breath, the Spirit has also been called living water.

The events that took place in Egypt when Joseph was a fellow prisoner with the king's wine steward and chief baker are profound. There, bread symbolized that which dies, and wine symbolized that which lives. This episode is special because there is a powerful lesson hidden in this ancient biblical event. It concerns the true Bread of Heaven.

In what could be the most strategic and revealing Scripture in the Bible, Jesus said, "The Spirit gives life; the flesh counts for nothing." John 6:63 NIV

We might paraphrase it this way: Bread dies, but wine lives when the wine is the blood of Christ.

If God had designed the world so that we could see spiritual beings, we would be able to see His eternal Spirit that dwells within us and combines with our human soul to give eternal life to our mortal selves.

Somewhere beyond the reach of test-tube evidence and the scope of human purview is God's spiritual biology, which holds His power of progeneration to imbue the souls of His children with eternal life.

This great symbolic teaching was acted out in real life in a dungeon in ancient Egypt. Two men were held in prison. One was like the body of John the Baptist. He was bread, and he died. The other was like the life-giving Spirit that John received at birth. He was wine and he lived. The symbolic natural part of John (the baker) died; the symbolic supernatural part of John (the butler) lived.

Just as Potiphar had trusted Joseph in his home, the warden of the prison put Joseph in charge. He paid no attention to anything under Joseph's care because the Lord was with Joseph and gave him success in whatever he did.

While Joseph was in prison, the Egyptian king became offended by his wine steward and his chief baker. Being incensed at his two courtiers, he had them arrested and placed in the same dungeon where Joseph was imprisoned. It became Joseph's responsibility to serve the two men who had fallen into trouble with their master.

Time passed, and one night both the wine steward and the baker had dreams. Their dreams were disturbing to them and seemed to have special meaning.

When Joseph saw them in the morning, it was obvious to him that they were upset. He asked the two deposed servants of the king, "Why do you look so worried today?"

"We have dreamed," they said. "Our dreams have us upset, and there is no one here to help us find the meaning."

Joseph told them that the interpretation of dreams belongs to God, and he asked the men to tell him the dreams.

The wine steward promptly said, "In my dream there was a grapevine right there in front of me. The vine had three branches, and as soon as its buds formed, its blossoms bloomed and its clusters ripened into grapes. Pharaoh's cup was in my hand, and I took the grapes and squeezed them into his cup. Then I placed the cup in Pharaoh's hand."

Joseph said, "This is the meaning of your dream: In three days the king will release you from prison and give back your position as wine server. You will again place Pharaoh's cup in his hand as you did before."

This pleased the butler, who thanked Joseph. The butler symbolized that part of the great precursor that did not die. And it fell upon the butler to become Joseph's precursor.

Joseph said, "Remember me when things go well for you. Remember that I was with you, and do me a favor and say something about me to Pharaoh. If you do this, you may get me out of this place. Tell him that I was originally kidnapped and ransomed from the land of Canaan, and I was brought to Egypt. I am not guilty of anything, and I do not deserve to be in this prison."

When the chief baker saw that Joseph's interpretation was good, he also asked him for an interpretation of his dream.

The chief baker said, "I saw myself in a dream. There were three baskets of excellent bread on my head. In the top basket there were several kinds of bread that Pharaoh eats. But birds were eating it from the basket on my head."

Joseph gave him the interpretation. He told him that the three baskets represented three days. Sadly, Joseph told him that in three days he would be hanged and that the birds would eat the flesh from his bones.

Both dreams came true in exactly the way Joseph interpreted them.

Jesus taught that anyone who has the Bread of Heaven, even though he should die, he will not die. He said it this way: "I am the resurrection and the life. He who believes in me will live, even though he dies." John 11:25 NIV

In that episode in the prison in ancient Egypt, the bread died, but the wine lived, and the wine was told to go ahead of Joseph and announce him to Pharaoh.

John the Baptist, the great precursor, about whom it was said, "I will send my messenger ahead of you, who will prepare your way before you" Matthew 11:10 NIV, was born filled with the Holy Spirit, so from birth he was both bread and wine. Herod arrested him and put him in prison, where the bread was killed, but the wine lived.

The great high language of God has allowed His beloved creatures to live free as their lives became woven into masterful mosaics of prophecy.

Extravagance and Glory

C.H. lived comfortably in the palace and worked as part of the king's food service. There was a large staff, some living in the intimate quarters of the palace while others were assigned to working jobs that kept them away from the intimate quarters.

Besides the king's wife there were other women living in the palace. Some had work assignments, while others were for entertainment only. All male servants living in the intimate quarters of the palace were eunuchs.

C.H. was very apprehensive about his condition, and he tried hard to be inconspicuous. That was difficult because one of the king's favorite people was a tattooed dancer whose eyes seemed to follow him everywhere he went.

"You must come with me," said Phygsis, who had been searching for C.H. "Pharaoh has dismissed all the other attendants and he told me to summon you for a private meeting. He said he wants no interruptions, nor does he want any other person entering the throne room under any circumstances while he meets with you."

Good grief, what's up? thought C.H. as he followed the steward.

Phygsis led C.H. to the lower-level entrance of the throne room, where a platoon of spear bearers stood guard. He stopped at the foot of the massive steps that led up to the throne. "Climb the steps all the way to the throne and bow the knee. The king will talk with you there."

C.H. gulped. This was highly unusual. He'd been told about the strict protocol in the royal throne room that determined how many steps a person could climb to speak to the king.

If the king agreed to speak with a commoner, that person could climb three steps, and the king would descend to that level and speak with him. Others could climb according to their status of importance. Only the most high-ranking persons could climb the entire seventy steps to the throne.

When Phygsis told him to climb all seventy steps to speak with the king, C.H. knew something was up.

He nervously climbed the steps all the way to the throne, where he dropped to his knees and bowed to the king.

The king sat regally upon his throne, exuding a spirit of superiority. The Egyptians believed him to be a god, and his pride elevated his ego to match their belief. He wore a princely dress, girded with a golden ephod that sparkled with many jewels, including a huge, dazzling ruby, an emerald, and a deep red carbuncle, all set in gold. Upon his head was a crown covered with more precious jewels. The throne upon which he sat was covered with gold, silver, and onyx. On his hands he wore many rings, and around his neck was a golden necklace.

"You wish to see me?" C.H. asked, his voice shaking a bit.

"Yes," said the king. "You have been in my food service for a few years, is that right?" The king did not wait for an answer. "Information has come to me that you have many talents, and that you are quite an expert in certain things."

"I'm a journalist," said C.H. "I guess you'd call me a scribe."

"Do you enjoy living in my house?" asked the king as he looked C.H. in the eye for the first time.

"It's OK," said C.H., his apprehension growing.

"You do a fine job in food service," said the king. "But it has come to my ears that you have another talent. I hear you are an expert at robbing graves."

The statement hit C.H. like a surprise left hook to the jaw.

"How amazing, to have an expert grave robber living in my house." The king gave C.H. a squinty-eyed stare under heavy black eyeliner. "That is a crime punishable by death, you know."

C.H. felt as if the king's eyes were actually piercing him. He began to sweat.

"I am told you have many years of experience, and that you have laid up riches, yet you have never been caught. What a sleuth you must be! Such a clever man now passes as a slave in my palace food service. Why is that?"

Without permitting a reply, Pharaoh continued. "I believe you are a fake. You are living in my house dishonestly. Tell me, have you had the required surgery to be qualified to live in the intimate quarters of my house? Are you really a eunuch?"

C.H. was silent.

"That is what I thought. And that is why I have a special assignment for you. Would you like to redeem yourself, save your life, and gain my favor?"

"H–How may I serve you?" stuttered C.H. as he felt sweat glistening on his face.

"You may serve me in a most important and secret manner," said the king in a deadly serious tone. "You must successfully complete the assignment you are given, and you must do so with the utmost discretion. Your very life depends upon how secret this matter is kept."

C.H. swallowed hard.

"Only the two of us will know of the things you are required to do. Should a third person ever hear of this matter, regardless of how it was learned, you and that person will both be hanged."

C.H. studied the king. His eyes seemed to have hardened and the makeup grown blacker. He knew he was in trouble. When he had first come to the palace to work, there was much whispering about two food service men who were sent to prison. One was later released; the other was hanged.

"My beloved stepmother, Hatshepsut, disappeared from this earth, and her corpse has never been found. Many search teams have failed to find her. I only know that she is securely buried and that the gods are blessing her."

C.H. had heard about the female king, and now he was to become part of her story.

Hatshepsut, the stepmother of Tutmosis III, was the fifth ruler of the eighteenth dynasty. Her father was Tutmosis I, and her mother was Queen Ahmose.

Hatshepsut was a beautiful, power-hungry woman, and she gained power in a rather high-handed way. Her half-brother, Tutmosis II, was Pharaoh of Egypt. As it was common for royal families to marry within the family, Tutmosis II married his half-sister Hatshepsut.

The rift between Hatshepsut and Tutmosis III was a family matter pertaining to his birthright. Tutmosis III was the son of her husband, Tutmosis II, but he was born of a despised second wife, a woman named after Isis, the goddess of fertility.

Tutmosis III's mother, Isis, like his grandmother, Moutnofritk, was a woman without noble blood. Therefore, his jealous stepmother (and half-aunt) referred to the illegitimate Tutmosis III as a bastard. She did not believe that he should be in line to become king.

Hatshepsut had no children by Tutmosis II, but she had two daughters, Nefrure and Meryetre, by a lover. She felt that Nefrure, the elder, was of more noble blood than Tutmosis III because Egyptians believed that the royal blood of the woman was more pure than that of a man.

Tutmosis II died in 1479 B.C. after a few short years as king. Being ill and fearing death, and knowing of Hatshepsut's power-hungry nature, he declared that ten-year-old Tutmosis III, who was serving as a priest of Amun, would be next in line to be king.

When Tutmosis II died, Hapuseneb, the high priest of Amun, with the support of other priests, appointed Hatshepsut to be the regent of the boy king Tutmosis III. At his coronation the young king was married to his half-sister Nefrure.

The widowed stepmother dominated the deceased king's young son and heir. Tutmosis III was king, but Hatshepsut usurped his ruling power. This lasted for about two years, until she became powerful enough to declare herself Pharaoh. Hapuseneb and other powerful priests gave their full support to Hatshepsut, and she ruled over Egypt as king, wearing a fake beard and men's clothing.

The kingdom grew weak under Hatshepsut, and her enemies became a growing danger at Egypt's borders.

During his time under Hatshepsut, Tutmosis III's character hardened. He spent most of his time in the army, and he became the commander-in-chief of the army at an early age.

Tutmosis III changed Egypt's standing in the world. History has identified him as the Napoleon of Egypt because he was such a fierce warrior. He led a force of 20,000 men against Gaza, Yaham, Megiddo, Tyre, Byblos, Sumur, Kadesh, Abel, and Abet. He was victorious in fifteen war campaigns. He gained and held absolute power in both the northern and southern kingdoms of Egypt.

Fifteen years after his coronation, the angry young king led a revolt against Hatshepsut. The end of her reign came swiftly.

When she was overthrown, Hatshepsut took a secret hiatus and was never seen nor heard from since.

The young Tutmosis III set upon a tirade of jealousy against her glory and her memory. Hatshepsut had glorified herself in lavish ways, filling the land with shrines, statues, obelisks, and reliefs. She had built her most magnificent temple at Deir el Bahari in Thebes near Luxor in the Valley of the Kings.

All the extravagant things that had been built to glorify Hatshepsut challenged Tutmosis III. He set out to rid the land of them all. But his anger and jealousy went even further. He wanted to find her dead body and spoil her corpse to ensure that she would have no glory or power in the afterlife.

C.H. was clearly being thrust into the center of a very emotional family matter. He knew little of the relationships or events that had brought him to his meeting with the king, but the veteran journalist could sense the seething anger in the king and the deeply passionate agenda that was unfolding before him.

There's something incendiary here, he thought.

"I wish I could give you some advice about how to find her," said the king, "but I cannot. That is why your expertise is important, and why you must dedicate yourself to this task."

"Your Majesty, tell me what things you wish me to do," replied C.H., "and I'll do my best to accomplish them."

"Listen carefully," said the king, lowering his voice. "I want the corpse of my beloved Hatshepsut to be found. All I can tell you is that she has been buried in an extravagant and splendid way in a secret tomb where no one can find her. She has been buried with treasure of all kinds and food for her afterlife. Her body has been preserved by embalmers, and she is lying face up in the burial chamber."

Tutmosis frowned. "You must find her and carefully turn her over, placing her face down."

The king leaned forward, and his words were like daggers. "Do you understand? She is to be face down."

He relaxed slightly. "Leave everything else exactly as it is, and steal nothing for yourself. But bring me something I will recognize from her tomb. Bring a small item that can be secreted in your clothing so it will not be noticed. I know all her precious belongings, and I will recognize whatever you bring."

"How will I find her?" asked C.H.

The king jumped to his feet and threw his hands into the air. "You disappoint me," he shouted. "If you are unprepared to accept this challenge, I can hang you this very hour. You are guilty of high crimes, you know."

C.H.'s adrenaline and his mind were racing at full throttle. He stood to his feet and faced the king. "I am an expert. I can do this thing, and not a soul in this world will know what I have done except you. Give me one hundred days and I will return to your satisfaction."

"Very well. You have one hundred days," said the king, momentarily becoming somewhat calmer. "Tell Phygsis that you are going shopping for the king, and he will supply your needs."

C.H. could hardly wait to get out of the presence of Tutmosis. When he was well away from the throne room, his body sagged. He felt as if he had just drowned again, and he gasped for breath as he staggered through the palace toward his quarters.

"What am I gonna do now?" he muttered.

He did not see the shadow that darted toward him, but he felt a hand grasp him by the arm. It was Phygsis. He led C.H. to a quiet, private place and told him to sit down and try to be calm.

After a long moment of silence, Phygsis said, "I know."

"You know what?" asked C.H.

"I know about your meeting with Tutmosis." After another long moment of silence, Phygsis whispered, "Meet me today at sundown in the byway beyond the palace on the west." Then he quietly disappeared.

At sundown C.H. stood in the designated byway. He shivered and waited nervously.

"I think I have a fever," he muttered. "What the heck? This is just another way to die."

C.H. grew despondent as his mind searched for some way out of this new predicament. He repeated aloud to himself some words he remembered from a conversation with the angel about the Bread of Heaven: "Even though you die, you will not die." He was learning to treasure those words.

He sighed. "I really need the Bread of Heaven. I'm in a real mess, and so is Joseph. I'm gonna die in Egypt. And there's no way ol' Tutmosis is gonna share his power with a little sheepherder."

After an hour of waiting, C.H. was ready to give up. Dragging his feet, he shuffled back toward the palace. But in the growing darkness he saw some figures approaching. As they came closer he recognized Phygsis riding in a horse-drawn chariot with two animals trailing. One was a mule carrying a large pack. The other was a donkey with no pack.

"Get in," said Phygsis.

C.H. got in, and they rode an hour's distance from the palace. As they rode, Phygsis explained that the chariot had been one of Hatshepsut's custom chariots, and it was being drawn by one of her special mules, with another mule from her stable serving as a pack animal. The donkey was for Phygsis' return trip to the palace.

The chariot had two wheels, each with six spokes, and a bench seat for two, with a rear basket for water, food, and clothing. At one time the chariot had been decorated with gold, silver, and precious stones, but those had all been removed.

"This is a good place," Phygsis said. "Let's stop here and cook some food. I brought some things from the palace. We'll camp here for the night."

They tethered the mules and built a small fire, on which Phygsis cooked supper. He also brought out some wine.

As they finished eating, Phygsis said, "You are the seventh."

"What do you mean?" asked C.H.

"Six men have been hanged because they could not find Hatshepsut's grave. You will be the seventh because you won't be able to find it either."

C.H. sat there quietly. Finally, he said, "This is supposed to be a secret. How do you know about it?"

"I'm the one who started the rumor that you are an expert grave robber. I knew the rumor would get back to Tutmosis."

"You what?" cried C.H. "That's the most ridiculous thing I've ever heard. Why would you do that?"

"It is a long story," said Phygsis.

They sat by the fire and talked for hours. Phygsis told C.H. that he had been a goldsmith before Hatshepsut made him a slave. He had made a beautiful golden medallion with a golden chain. "That was twenty-five years ago."

He told C.H. that the female king, who looked and acted like a man, saw Phygsis' wife wearing the beautiful golden medallion about her neck at a fish market in Memphis where the family was shopping.

"That is where the trouble started," he said.

Hatshepsut instantly fell in love with the medallion and tried to buy it. When the wife, who felt great sentimental value for her medallion, refused to sell it, the king became enraged and ordered her killed.

"Good grief!" said C.H. "That queen was one bad lady."

"King," said Phygsis. "She was king."

The king took the medallion, then arrested Phygsis and his young daughter and took them to the palace.

Phygsis was turned into a eunuch. He was motivated to be a good slave because he could live in the palace and be near his daughter, whom Hatshepsut had decided to claim as her own. She named the girl Isis after Tutmosis' mother.

"You see, I have two jobs," said Phygsis. "I am also the king's goldsmith. Did you see his signet ring and the medallion he wears about his neck? The king has a great treasure in jewelry that I have made for him."

Phygsis told C.H. how Hatshepsut schemed to match his daughter with Tutmosis III when they were children. She believed that a son of an ignoble mother deserved an ignoble wife. She also figured she could find a way to degrade the nobility of Tutmosis III and put her own daughter in line to be queen.

"You mean to tell me that tattooed dancer, Isis, is your daughter?" asked C.H.

"Yes," said Phygsis, looking intently at C.H. "I have watched you when you notice her. She arouses you, and that has put both your life and hers in great danger. Even worse, her eyes follow you everywhere, and she knows you are not a eunuch. That is why I had to start the rumor about your being a grave robber."

Phygsis told C.H. that for the past twenty-five years he had been a special servant, gaining respect and power. He had served the royal family through a whole generation. "I watched Tutmosis grow up," said Phygsis.

"Has the king ever asked you to find the grave of Hatshepsut?" C.H. asked.

"No. I think old relationships have held him back. But I know the day is coming. If you are the seventh man hanged, I will surely be the eighth. But you see, I know where the body is buried, and I can find it and do his dirty deed."

"If you know where the body is," C.H. said, "then why not tell him?"

"At this late date? He would hang me for keeping the secret. I should have volunteered the information when he first started looking for her. Now it is too late, and he will not forgive me."

"So where is it?"

"It is in Punt."

"Where the blue blazes is Punt?"

"Outside of Egypt, near the horn of Africa. Hatshepsut used to go on shopping trips there. I often accompanied her. On the largest expedition, the great Senenmet led us in five ships." Phygsis leaned back and reflected. "Each of the five ships had thirty rowers. They were from Qoseir, on the Red Sea. That was in the eighth year of her reign. We brought back myrrh, frankincense, and fragrant unguents. Punt was called God's land."

"Hold it one minute," said C.H., interrupting Phygsis' reminiscing. "My life is at stake here. How do you know the queen…king…is buried in this Punt place?"

"I built the tomb, and I placed her body in it. It was difficult, but I had help. All those who helped me are now dead, so I am the only one left who knows where she is buried."

Phygsis' remarks rang like a fire alarm in the journalist's ears. Only one person alive knew the location of the lady king's tomb. And now he had revealed that secret to someone else.

"You are a faithful servant," C.H. said to Phygsis, hoping to hide his growing suspicions toward this man who may have blood on his hands. "But are your loyalties more to the dead than to the living?"

"Loyalties?" repeated Phygsis in a raised voice. "My wife is dead, but at least she does not have to suffer the embarrassment of seeing her daughter as a tattooed dancer who performs naked before the king. My daughter would be safer, happier, and living better if Hatshepsut were still king. I was Hatshepsut's trusted slave and confidant. She honored me by making my daughter's life safe and pleasant."

Phygsis spent the next few hours explaining to C.H. how to find Hatshepsut's grave site. "Here, I have drawn a map for you."

Phygsis handed C.H. a hand-drawn map. "Her beloved highness was very worried about her burial. Pyramids do not provide security for the dead or their treasures. Tomb robbers are persistent and cunning. Valuables from almost every pyramid in Egypt have been stolen. That is why rock-cut tombs have became popular in recent years."

"What is a rock-cut tomb?" C.H. asked.

"It is a cavernous area carved into a natural rock setting. To deceive and confuse would-be tomb robbers, it contains false doors, misdirecting tunnels, unexpected changes of direction, blocked passages, and sealed entrances. About sixty rock-cut tombs have been built in the Valley of the Kings at Thebes."

"Is that the kind of tomb you made for Hatshepsut?"

"We considered it. But then, on one of her expeditions to Punt, we saw a new, large granary that was nearing completion. When a landslide came down and covered it completely, she decided to erect a shrine to the god Ptah over the buried granary. The cavernous granary that lay below the shrine could be secretly excavated and prepared for her tomb. That would provide the perfect deception."

"Clever," C.H. said. "A sacred place respecting a god would not attract grave robbers."

"The granary had been built of limestone and granite," explained Phygsis. "The builders had tried getting granite from a quarry south of Punt, but the people there are bad. Ptah created them out of the black mud that boils up out of the ground."

C.H. snorted. "The Bible says that's how God created Adam and Eve." He scratched his head, trying to remember the details. "If I recall correctly, Moses wrote Genesis, which has the story about Adam and Eve. But, as we sit here, Moses is still about four hundred years in the future. Man, this ancient stuff is weird. Anyway, I guess you wouldn't have heard about Adam and Eve."

Phygsis ignored C.H.'s ramblings and continued his story. "The builders floated the granite down the Nile from a quarry in Aswan. When they entered the sea, they turned their ships westward and headed for Punt. Bad weather came upon one ship and it became lost. It passed through the Pillars of Melqart and fell off the face of the earth, where it was destroyed by dragons."

"That's prehistoric baloney," C.H. said. "Your Pillars of Melqart must be the Straits of Gibraltar. But there aren't any dragons out there. The world is round, man." C.H. slapped his forehead with his open palm.

Still ignoring C.H.'s remarks, Phygsis asked, "How many days did the king give you to fulfill your task?"

"One hundred," replied C.H.

"That's barely enough time," said Phygsis, shaking his head. "If you maintain a good pace and rotate the mules from pack to chariot, you should reach the shrine in twenty to thirty days. After reaching the tomb, you may need four or five days to enter the tomb if you follow my instructions. It will be enough time if you do not waste a minute."

Phygsis stood. "I must leave now. I need to return to the palace. I suggest you get some rest and then get an early start." Phygsis mounted the donkey and left.

C.H. studied the map in the early morning light. "This is crazy. I don't understand hieroglyphics. My African geography isn't that fresh, but I'd say this looks like Libya."

C.H. set out on the long, torturous trip. He traveled by chariot beyond Egypt. He met a couple of strangers along the way and asked them about Punt, but neither of them had ever heard of the place. Once he saw a caravan in the distance, but it moved out of sight, in the opposite direction from his presumed course.

As the weary days passed, supplies ran low and fatigue set in. C.H. became desperate and frightened. His hope began to fade.

Finally, C.H. sat on a stump, folded his arms, and rocked back and forth, moaning and groaning and making incoherent sounds. He tried counting the days he had traveled, but his mind was too foggy.

"Phygsis said not to waste a minute," he muttered. "But where is this Punt place? I've been following this stupid map for a hundred days already, and now I'm stuck in this barren place. There's no shrine here."

C.H. threw the map away in disgust. He was tired, dirty, disheveled, hungry, and disgruntled. "What am I doing anyway, searching for a dead body just to turn it over and place it face down? How dumb is that?

"Then again, what are my choices? I can die here or go back to the king and get hung. Or I could go back to my old life where I am already dead. In any case I'm never going to find the Bread of Heaven. I'm going to be dead forever." He began to cry with great body-shaking sobs.

C.H. rotated his mules again, then decided to head back to Egypt. But before he climbed back into the chariot, he got down on his knees.

With his face against the ground, he prayed in desperation. "Dear God, please help me. Show me this place called Punt."

No great sign appeared. So C.H. got into the chariot and started driving. After a moment he looked up and realized he was driving down a path in a strange, mysterious community built at the foot of some mountains. There were thatched houses shaped like beehives, built high above the ground on stilts. People scurried around everywhere, all busily going about their daily tasks.

"This has to be Punt," C.H. cried out. "It looks just like Phygsis described it. Now we're getting somewhere. But where the heck is the shrine of Ptah?"

"It is no longer visible," said a voice next to him.

Startled, C.H. almost jumped out of the chariot. But when he turned to look, he saw his angel, Helper. "You scared me out of my wits," he hollered. "What are you doing here?"

"You prayed to the Lord God," replied the angel. "You should pray more often when you are in need."

C.H. rolled his eyes.

"The shrine of Ptah was there," said the angel, pointing to an area on the side of a large hill. "Like the granary that lies beneath it, the shrine has been covered by a landslide."

C.H. could not see a shred of evidence that anything lay beneath the huge pile of earth that had come down from the hill above. "I might as well have died in the desert. There's no way I'm going to get into some dark chamber hidden under that mountain. Besides, my hundred days are up. It's too late."

The angel stepped down from the chariot. "Follow me."

Instantly, C.H. found himself in the cavernous tomb of Hatshepsut. It was illuminated by the light of God emanating from Helper.

"Wow!" said C.H.

In the center of the huge tomb, nestled between four pillars, was a raised platform, about waist high, like a square island. A mummified body lay face up on it. The corpse looked like a centerpiece in a huge, elaborate castle.

Stored in the tomb with her was a great supply of grain, foods, and personal items. There were no doors or windows and no apparent way in or out. The air was stale. There was total silence. The place reminded C.H. of a bomb shelter, except the ceiling was very high.

"Wow," he repeated.

With an eerie feeling C.H. slowly walked around the platform, never taking his eyes off the dead form of Hatshepsut. He stared at the body in awe and stepped as if he were walking on eggs.

In a barely audible whisper, he spoke to the corpse. "Can you save me from the gallows?"

Overcome, C.H. fell to his knees and put his head on the floor of the tomb. He prayed to the angel, thanking him for leading him here and asking him to help him choose a token from the tomb to take back to appease Tutmosis.

When C.H. stood, the angel raised his hand like an officer stopping traffic. "Never pray to an angel, and do not presume to speak to the dead. Only prayers that are directed to the Most High can be heard."

"Yeah, I knew that. Sorry. I also know I should have been praying when I was out there trying to read that stupid map. Now it's too late. The king gave me one hundred days, and those days are gone. I'm going to be hung."

"You're wrong," said the angel. "It has not been a hundred days since you spoke with the king. You lost count."

"Really?" exclaimed C.H. His stooped shoulders jerked upright. "That's great! Maybe I've got a chance."

"Your friend deceived you," said the angel.

"You mean Phygsis?"

The angel nodded.

"Why would he lie to me?" he asked. "He's fearful for his own life."

"No," said the angel. "He has no fear for his life. His loyalty to Hatshepsut remains strong. His plan has always been to protect the former Pharaoh's chance for a glorious afterlife."

"But why would he start a crazy rumor about me, and then lie to me about it?"

"His daughter. He is afraid for her. She has become attracted to you, and that puts her life in danger."

"Was everything he told me a lie?"

"No. Much of it was true. Some was not. He was just trying to protect those he loves."

"Oh, come on, Helper. I didn't do a thing to that tattooed girl. Sure, I looked at her. Who wouldn't, with a body like that and nearly naked? She does a heck of a dance."

"The interest you showed in her gave her the impression that you have feelings for her, and she developed feelings for you," explained the angel. "Her father wanted you far away from her. The map was designed for your destruction. He wanted to send you far away forever."

"So the whole thing was a setup," growled C.H. "I'll show him a thing or two. Maybe I'll just think up a little scheme of my own."

"The Lord God wants you to forgive him," said the angel.

"No way, man," retorted C.H. "He needs his butt kicked."

"If you want your prayers answered, you must forgive."

C.H. walked around the corpse of Hatshepsut, trying to get a hold on his feelings. Forgiving was not his thing. But he knew the angel was telling the truth about forgiveness.

"Why is it so important to the king that I turn her dead body over and have her face down?"

"Like most Egyptians, the king believes that every person is composed of three life elements: body, ba, and ka."

"Say that again?"

"He believes that the body is the physical part of the person, and the ba and the ka are the spiritual parts. According to his pagan religion, the ba of Hatshepsut is her character and personality. It appears as a bird with a human head, which flies around continuously inside this tomb."

C.H. ducked down and turned his head in every direction, looking for some birdlike figure.

"Do not worry," said the angel. "There is no bird in this tomb. The king is wrong and his religion is false."

C.H. relaxed, but only a little.

"The king also believes each person has a ka. The ka is the life force. When you have it, you are alive, and when you do not have it, you are dead. If Hatshepsut's ka reconnects with her body, she will have an afterlife, with all her beauty and glory. But if the ka does not reconnect with the body, she will not have an afterlife. The food that was left here is for the ka. The ka would never actually eat this food, but it would partake of its life-giving essence."

"I still don't understand why he wants her face down," said C.H.

"Centuries of Egyptian kings have gone to a great deal of trouble to preserve their bodies because they believed the ka cannot re-enter the body if it cannot recognize it," said the angel.

"So if Hatshepsut's body is turned face down," said C.H., "her ka will not be able to recognize her and she will have no afterlife?"

"That is the idea," said the angel. "If the ka recognizes her and returns to her, that will also permit the ba to stop flying around the tomb and return to the body. When the body reconnects with the ba and the ka, the combination is called the akh."

"That jealous son of a gun," yelled C.H. "He wants me to kill his mother's chances of an afterlife. If I turn her body over, she'll be dead forever."

C.H. stared at Hatshepsut's corpse and backed away from it slowly. "But she's already dead. Just like I am. We both need the Bread of Heaven."

C.H. turned to the angel. "I'm not a hit man. How can I do such a dreadful thing? How can I spoil Hatshepsut's afterlife?"

"You can do nothing to help her, nor can you do anything to harm her," said the angel. "Her afterlife is not in the hands of false gods. The Egyptian concept of an afterlife is all vanity, and the religion of the ba, the ka, and the akh is a false religion. Turning the body over or leaving it face up is of no importance."

"What should I do?"

"Keep your mind and heart on things that are just and true."

"What things are those?" asked C.H.

"No mortal will enter God's rest unless he belongs to Him, and no one can belong to Him unless he has the Bread of Heaven. There are no exceptions. No eye has seen and no mind has conceived the glorious afterlife of those who have the Bread of Heaven."

C.H. stared at the corpse. "I wonder where she will be in eternity," he mused.

"She is in the hands of God," said the angel.

C.H. gave a long sigh. Then he began looking for a way to climb up on the superstructure where Hatshepsut's body lay.

"Since it won't affect her afterlife, I might as well do what Tutmosis asked."

When he had scaled the platform, he stood quietly for a moment and looked at all the treasures glistening around him. "Such extravagance," he muttered. "I wish I owned all this gold."

C.H. looked at the corpse. "I guess she plans on being a man in her afterlife. She's still wearing a fake beard. She's also wearing a golden medallion around her neck. Hey! That's got to be the one Phygsis said he made. That's the little trinket that got his wife killed."

He carefully removed the medallion from the corpse, then stood and showed it to the angel. "Look! I did it!" he exclaimed. "I've got the golden medallion. That should prove to the king that I did what he asked."

C.H. slung the treasure around his own neck. Then he took hold of the corpse and carefully and slowly began to turn it over. It was surprisingly light, and C.H. had no trouble completing the task. After the gruesome job was finished, he scrambled back down to the floor of the tomb.

He looked at the angel. "OK, I did this dirty thing. Now, I just have one question that's bothering me."

"What's that?" asked the angel.

"I'm looking for points of congruency, right?"

"Correct."

"Well, I don't see how Tutmosis fits," said C.H. "Joseph fits. He's the perfect model of the perfect Man. But where is the congruency between Tutmosis and God?"

"Let me ask you a question about Tutmosis," said the angel.

"OK, shoot," said C.H.

"Does the king hold great power in Egypt?"

"Absolutely! He holds the power of life and death over every man, woman, child, and horse in Egypt."

"Do the Egyptians believe him to be a god?"

"Yes."

"Has he conquered all his enemies?"

"Like a mighty warrior," answered C.H. "He has conquered almost the whole world."

"Does Tutmosis discriminate?" asked the angel.

"Try climbing seventy steps to the throne when you are not invited. Or get caught living in his palace without the required surgery. Yeah, he discriminates," said C.H.

"When Pharaoh declares himself to be the one and only sovereign king, would he be happy to hear rumors of another?"

"Of course not."

"When Jesus' disciples wanted to worship Him, He told them that He did not seek glory, but there is One who does seek glory."

"Yeah," said C.H. "The Father."

"Does Tutmosis seek glory?"

"In extreme measure. He builds huge structures, statues, reliefs, and all kinds of other things to glorify himself."

"Is he jealous?" asked the angel.

"Yeah, his jealousy has destroyed half of Egypt. He is the most jealous of all."

"Except the Lord God," the angel retorted. "God is more jealous than anyone who has ever existed. He said His very name is Jealous."

"OK, I guess those things are true. But it's hard for me to think of Tutmosis as having a lot of godly traits. I mean, what about love? Where's the love?"

"Have you forgotten that this story started in Canaan?" asked the angel. "Did Jacob not love his family? How many earthly men should it take to model the Creator?"

CHAPTER 10

The Search

"Follow me," said the angel.

As suddenly as C.H. had discovered himself inside the tomb, he now found himself outside. He happily breathed fresh air while standing beside the angel on the palace grounds.

"Wow! This smells better. I now know that all things are possible with—" He turned to look at the angel, but Helper was gone.

As he approached the palace C.H. became cautious. Something unusual was happening. Crowds of people covered the palace grounds. Some stood in groups talking.

"What the heck?" he muttered.

Strange people of all kinds were there—people he had not seen before. They stood or sat in small groups talking. Some wore priestly attire.

One man in particular caught C.H.'s attention. He wore a lot of fur and a fake tail.

When he entered the palace C.H. went directly to the throne room, hoping to speak to the king. Throne-room protocol was obviously suspended. People were at various places on the steps leading to the throne.

Some people were coming down and some were climbing. There was a small group near the throne in a conversation with the king.

Normal protocol dictated that no one could enter the throne room without Phygsis' permission. Now, something different was happening.

"Something's up," he said to himself.

As C.H. climbed the steps to the throne, he saw Phygsis near the king with several other attendants. Phygsis caught a glimpse of C.H. out of the corner of his eye, and his body jerked as he did a full double-take. His reaction was total shock.

He expected me to die in the wilderness, C.H. thought. *Now he probably thinks I've come back to surrender myself and get hung.*

Wearing his best poker face C.H. walked right past the astonished Phygsis, who was too confused to try to stop him from approaching the throne.

Like my ol' daddy taught me: Use the element of surprise. Nefrure, the king's wife, was there with several of her attendants. A platoon of archers and ax warriors stood behind the throne.

As C.H. approached the group near the throne, he stopped abruptly and jumped back with surprise. There were three creatures talking with the king. Each creature had the body of a man and a bare upper body and bare legs. One had the head of a jackal, one had the head of a vulture, and the other had the head of a hawk.

The king finished talking with the three creatures and dismissed them. As they left, the creature with the head of a jackal brushed against C.H.

"What the heck was that?" C.H. wondered out loud.

"That was the god Anubis," replied Phygsis, who had positioned himself nearby and clutched C.H.'s elbow.

He could tell from the tug on his elbow that Phygsis wanted him to leave and not see the king. But Tutmosis looked up and saw C.H.

The king did not seem surprised to see him, and he called for him to come before the throne. In the same manner as his previous visit,

C.H. bowed before the king. Phygsis and Nefrure both stood close by, and no one was asked to leave the throne room.

There was an awkward silence while C.H. and the king looked at each other.

"Did you come to be hanged?" Phygsis asked.

Where's the secrecy? C.H. wondered. *I thought this mater was supposed to be between me and the king.*

C.H. glanced at Nefrure, then at Phygsis, and finally back at the king. He was about to speak when Tutmosis asked, "Did you find the tomb?"

Apparently, what had been secret was no longer secret.

"Yes."

"Where is your proof?"

C.H. reached into his garment and withdrew the golden medallion he had taken from Hatshepsut's corpse. He handed it to the king.

When Phygsis saw the golden medallion, a gust of astonishment burst from him, and he quickly left the throne room.

Tutmosis' face showed instant recognition. He had undoubtedly seen it many times around Hatshepsut's neck.

Nefrure squealed and grabbed the medallion from the king. "Where did you get this?"

The king acted distracted and indifferent. He should explain things to his wife. Instead he changed the subject abruptly and said, "I had a dream."

C.H. was caught off guard. He wanted his victory, but now the king wanted to talk about a dream.

While C.H. had been hunting for Hatshepsut's tomb, Pharaoh had been having troubling dreams. His furrowed brow and somber demeanor showed how disturbed he was over the dream.

"I need an interpretation," said the king.

"That explains the crowds," said C.H. snapping his fingers. "Of course! That's what all these people are doing here." His memory was triggered. He recalled asking the angel if this was the king who dreamt of the cows.

"Yeah, I remember hearing something about cows," he muttered.

C.H. looked around at those attending the king. They all wore solemn expressions.

"All of my people are searching for wise men," said the king. "They are going about the land, summoning any who might be able to interpret my dreams."

C.H. looked at the man sitting on the throne of Egypt in wonderment. The king looked and acted like a changed man. It was evident that he had a profound mystery sealed up in his mind. He needed an inspired person with powerful discernment and insight to break the mystery of his dream and open its meaning.

"God gave you the dream," blurted C.H.

Pharaoh told his dream to C.H. When he finished, he sat back in a slump. He was weary from repeating the same thing over and over.

Pharaoh took the medallion from Nefrure and handed it back to C.H. "I believe this belongs to a thief." He looked at C.H. and said, "You have proven your expertise, but you will rob no more tombs."

The king stood in a show of honor to C.H. "And now, I, Pharaoh, want to reward you. I know you are not a eunuch. I will give you any woman you may choose from my palace."

Nefrure gasped when she heard that C.H. was not a eunuch.

C.H. gave no response. He took the golden medallion and left. When he had departed the throne room and was walking toward his quarters, he noticed from the corner of his eye that Phygsis was following him. He began to walk faster, only to see that Phygsis was also walking faster.

OK, let's find out what's cooking, thought C.H. He stopped to let Phygsis catch up. *His curiosity is killing him, but I'm not giving him a clue. Let him stew in it.*

"Hey, Phygsis, what's your hurry? Why aren't you helping the king with all this crowd?"

"Nefrure is there, and I will only be gone a minute," replied Phygsis.

Phygsis had a lot to lose. He had betrayed both C.H. and the king.

I think he's playing defense, C.H. thought.

Phygsis' demeanor was changed. He looked like a defeated man who could not accept his loss. C.H. could feel his curiosity.

He had forgiven Phygsis, but he couldn't resist a wisecrack. "Drawn any good maps lately?"

As Phygsis stood there, he gave C.H. the mental image of a guilty dog with its tail between its legs.

Finally, Phygsis said, "Wow! Did you hear the king say you can choose any woman in the palace, and she will be yours? He knows you are not a—"

"You scoundrel. You were eavesdropping," said C.H. "I thought you left the throne room before the king and I talked."

"No, no, I was there," said Phygsis. Obviously, it was awkward for him, but he continued to try to have a conversation. "Any woman? Who will you choose?"

Hmm, thought C.H. *This is about his daughter again. What's he getting at? Maybe Pharaoh will hang them both.*

"I heard the king," replied C.H. "Now I have a question for you. There is a young slave named Joseph who belonged to a commander named Potiphar. Are you holding him in prison?"

"Why? Do you want him released?" asked Phygsis.

"Maybe."

"He is a Hebrew from Canaan. Yes, he is in prison, but only the king can release him."

C.H. took the golden medallion from his garment and looked at it carefully for the first time.

"Very good craftsmanship," he said, examining it with interest. He folded the medallion and chain in his right hand. With his left hand he took Phygsis' trembling hand and held it with the palm up. Then he put the golden medallion in Phygsis' hand.

"The true owner of that piece of jewelry is a widow named Mahti," said C.H. "She lives alone in Memphis, and she works in a fish market. Her husband and small daughter were killed by Hatshepsut many years ago."

C.H. was filled with compassion when he saw shock in the eyes of his nemesis. Phygsis stared at the medallion and tried to comprehend C.H.'s words.

The startling revelation plunged through his body like a blunt spear. He stood motionless for a moment and then started shaking and fell to his knees.

All these years he and his daughter, Isis, believed their wife and mother to be dead, and at the same time Mahti believed her husband and daughter were dead.

C.H. walked away and continued to his quarters.

During the dark of the night, both Phygsis and Isis disappeared, and no one knew where they went.

Merod's Testimony

Early the next morning the king summoned C.H. to the throne room. Pharaoh appeared quite frustrated. His mysterious dreams were sealed tightly in his mind and they were causing fear and anxiety.

"Phygsis is gone," said the king, throwing his arms into the air. "He disappeared during the night. You now have two jobs: yours and his."

The crowd around the palace had grown. They'd come to hear the king's dream. Servants were scurrying everywhere. The food service people were rounding up all kinds of people to hear the dream. The king's orders were absolute: let no one be overlooked.

"It is your job now," he told C.H. "Be about it! I want wise men to hear my dreams. Bring them from all the borders of Egypt."

"There's a big crowd here already."

"Anyone who tries to deceive me will die," the king warned.

"You have a young slave in prison who interprets dreams," C.H. told the king.

"Let's start with my commanders," Tutmosis said, obviously not interested in releasing a prisoner. "Bring my army commanders here. I will tell them my dream."

C.H. brought in a group of army commanders, and the king again told his dream. Their questions irritated him, but he gave diligence in revealing every detail.

It was obvious that the king was growing frustrated and short tempered. *What a drag,* thought C.H., *having to repeat the same thing over and over.*

The army commanders gave their thoughts and ideas to the king, and he shouted, "Out! Out, or I'll hang you."

C.H. quickly ushered the commanders out of the throne room. He said, "Stay close, we need to talk. The big guy is gonna blow his fuse if we're not careful. Somebody may get hung."

Then he went to the king and said, "Your Highness, I have a plan. Let me tell you a way your dreams can be heard by a large number of people. The crowd is growing, and it is becoming an impossible job for one person to repeat the dream so many times."

"Let me hear your plan," said the weary king.

"Also, Your Highness, I would again tell you that you have a young slave in prison who interprets dreams."

The king was anxious for a solution, so he approved C.H.'s plan, but he had disdain for releasing a criminal.

To implement his plan C.H. asked the army commanders to meet with him, and he put them through a drill. He had a rehearsal, with each of them taking turns repeating the king's dream.

When they were proficient in telling the king's dreams accurately, he assigned each of them a place where a group could gather and they could repeat the dreams to those who were to hear them. They would listen for valid opinions and bring all plausible interpretations to the king.

The routine became well practiced, and huge crowds of wise men, magicians, physicians, gods, priests, and important people from all over Egypt heard the king's dreams.

This continued for days because the search was very diligent, but no one was able to give an interpretation. Each day, as tension built,

C.H. reminded the king that a young slave was being held in prison who could interpret dreams.

"He can search to high heaven, and he is not going to find anyone to interpret his dreams until he releases Joseph," C.H. muttered. "And if it doesn't happen soon, heads are gonna get chopped."

Suddenly, an idea came to C.H. He walked while he talked to himself. "Why didn't I think of this before? Somewhere in the palace there may be a servant who knows about Joseph. I think he is a baker or something. He was in prison with another guy and they had dreams."

C.H. set out on a search of his own. "The sheepherder kid doesn't have a chance, but we might as well find a way for him to give it a shot."

There were workers in the bake shop, and there were workers on the roof of the bake shop where the ovens were.

C.H. spoke to a young man in the bake shop. "There was a palace baker who was put in prison with another guy, maybe a wine guy. The wine guy was hung and the baker was released. I'm looking for the guy who was released."

"Sir, I think you have it backwards. The late chief baker had the misfortune of being hung three years ago, and the chief wine steward was released. I think you are looking for Merod, the wine steward."

C.H. snapped his fingers. "Yeah, that's right." He turned on his heels and headed out to search for Merod. "Thanks," he yelled over his shoulder.

C.H. found the head wine steward and spoke to him about Joseph.

Merod said, "Oh, yes, now I remember my sins. I was to go ahead of him and tell of him."

C.H. didn't have a clue that, finally, the symbolism in ancient Egypt that foresaw John the Baptist, the great precursor of Christ who went before Him to announce Him, was consummated by Merod the wine steward.

C.H. quickly took him to the throne room, where he gave his testimony about Joseph's ability to interpret dreams.

Merod came before the king and bowed down to him. "May the king live forever and his glory be exalted in the land."

"Do you have testimony?" asked the king.

"Three years have passed since you were angry with your servant and placed me in the ward."

The king nodded that he remembered.

"I was in custody for some time with the chief of bakers, and we were confined with a Hebrew slave who attended us. We each dreamt a disturbing dream, and he gave us an interpretation, and not one of his words fell to the ground."

The king sat quietly with his arms folded, and there was a slight nod of his head.

"If it pleases the king, let him not slay the wise men and magicians of Egypt, but let him release the Hebrew and require of him the correct interpretation of the king's dreams," concluded Merod.

CHAPTER 12

Joseph Interprets the Dream

So Pharaoh sent for Joseph, who was brought from the dungeon. After he had shaved and changed clothes, Joseph, who was now thirty years old, came before Pharaoh.

C.H. remembered the angel's words about how he could witness prophetic things that would happen in the house of Tutmosis III. He had actually become part of the proceedings.

The throne room was cleared of all other candidates who had come to hear the king's dream. Throne room protocol was again in force.

The king descended to the fourth step and sat on it to speak with Joseph. Joseph ascended to the third step and bowed before the king.

The king was splendid in his princely attire and girded about with a golden ephod. His jewels sparkled and dazzled all who looked upon him. Joseph had never seen such a grand person, and he wondered greatly about the mighty king of Egypt.

Pharaoh said to Joseph, "I had a dream, and no one can interpret it. But I have heard that you can interpret dreams."

Joseph said, "I cannot do it, but God can give Pharaoh the answer he desires."

Tutmosis told Joseph his dream. "In my dream I was standing on the bank of the Nile when out of the river there came seven cows. They were fat and sleek and grazing among the reeds. They were followed by seven other cows, which were scrawny, ugly, and lean. Never were there such ugly cows in all the land of Egypt."

The king shifted his posture. He hesitated and lowered his voice. The next part of the dream was hard to tell because it sounded so preposterous.

"The lean cows ate the fat cows. But after they ate them, they looked just as ugly as before."

Joseph was a good audience, so Pharaoh continued. "I also saw seven ears of corn, full and good, growing on a single stalk. After them, seven other ears sprouted, but they were withered and thin and scorched by the east wind. The thin ears of corn swallowed up the seven good ears."

Pharaoh eyed Joseph intently, looking for clues that he may have an interpretation.

Joseph gave Pharaoh an affirmative nod. God had clothed him with the spirit of knowledge and understanding. He listened intently to Pharaoh's dreams, and when he had heard them Joseph said to Tutmosis, "Pharaoh's dreams are one and the same. Do not imagine that there are two dreams. God has revealed to Pharaoh what He is about to do."

Pharaoh, eager to hear, moved down from the fourth step to be closer to Joseph on the third step.

Joseph said, "The seven good cows are seven years, and the seven good ears of corn are seven years. They are the same dream."

Pharaoh's habit was to be abrupt when he heard anything that did not sound right to his ears. But he sat quietly, and Joseph continued.

"The seven ugly cows and the seven worthless ears of corn are the same. They represent seven years of famine."

Pharaoh tilted his head to one side as if it would help him hear and understand better. He remembered Merod's testimony about Joseph's ability to interpret dreams.

Joseph continued. "God has shown Pharaoh what He is about to do. Seven years of abundance are coming to the land of Egypt, but seven years of famine will follow them. When the lean years come, they will be so severe that the abundance in Egypt will be wiped out, and the famine will ravage the land."

Blood drained from Pharaoh's face. His mouth fell open, and his eyes got big. He knew he was hearing powerful words from God, and he sensed that all of Egypt would suffer.

Joseph said, "The reason the dream was given to Pharaoh in two forms is that the matter has been firmly decided by God, and He will do it soon."

Joseph spoke with godly wisdom to Pharaoh. He told Pharaoh to look for a discerning and wise man, and put him in charge of the land of Egypt.

He told Pharaoh to appoint commissioners over the land to take a fifth of the harvest of Egypt during the seven years of abundance. They should collect all the food of the good years that were coming and store up the grain under the authority of Pharaoh, to be kept in the cities for food.

Joseph explained that the food should be held in reserve for the country, to be used during the seven years of famine that would come upon Egypt, so that the country and all its people would not be destroyed by the famine.

C.H. listened to every word spoken by Joseph. His purpose was to look for symbolism and points of congruency. But he had no idea that Joseph's powerful words portended a much larger prophecy.

Joseph had parallel dreams, and now Pharaoh had parallel dreams. He dreamt of cows and of corn, and his dreams foretold of parallel famines. Neither Joseph nor Pharaoh had any reason to suspect that God's symbolism was upon them. The famine that came upon Egypt foreshadowed a great spiritual famine that would come upon the world in the last days.

As Joseph spoke, C.H. could not help but notice the contrast between the young shepherd from Canaan and the Egyptians. He was a young, inexperienced foreigner who did not look like the Egyptians. He wore no makeup or black eyeliner. He spoke with the accent of a Jew. His demeanor was humble and meek, but his words were powerful and forthright. He exuded faith because he spoke the words that God gave him. It all sounded good to Pharaoh.

The kid is a handsome dude, thought C.H. *I wonder if there is a chance for him after all.* His guts tied themselves into a knot. He felt like he had just bet his last two dollars on a hundred-to-one long shot.

"C'mon, King Tut," C.H. muttered to himself. "Give a dead man a break. The ba and the ka ain't gonna cut it. I want to live forever."

Tutmosis sent for all his officers, princes, nobles, advisors, servants, and all who lived in his house, and they all came before the king.

The king spoke to the assembly. "Behold, you have seen and heard all the words of this Hebrew man, and you have heard his wisdom, and you know Merod spoke the truth. None of the Hebrew's words fall to the ground."

The king continued. "You know that he has given a proper interpretation of the dream, and it will surely come to pass. Now, therefore, take counsel, and know what I must do and how the land will be delivered from the famine."

The people could hardly believe their ears. Never had this king shown any evidence of seeking counsel, nor had he ever given a hint that he might share his power.

"Seek now, also, whether anyone like this man can be found, in whom there is a heart of wisdom and knowledge," said the king.

"Our lord and king," they all said, "behold the whole land of Egypt from north to south is in your hand. Choose, therefore, whoever you find that has the wisdom to deliver the land from the devastation, and appoint him to be under the king and over the land."

Interesting advice, thought C.H. *"Under the king and over the land." That's got to be theological.*

"Gather all the people from the palace and all the people who are about on the grounds," said Pharaoh. "Gather them from all lands and areas around, and gather them in the courtyard. I will stand above them in the upper portico to my chambers, and I will speak to all the people."

C.H. sucked in a quick breath of optimism. This could be big!

All the people from Pharaoh's house, and all the people from the surrounding areas, and all the people who had been summoned from far-off places were gathered together in the large courtyard.

The commanders from the army were there, the priests were there, and the wise men and the magicians were there. The creatures who appeared like men with heads of jackals or hawks or vultures were there. Those who wore fake tails and feathered bodies were there.

CHAPTER 13

The Coronation

When the people were all gathered, Pharaoh stood on a large balcony in the upper portico that led to his chambers and looked down upon them. He had Joseph standing next to him, and he raised his arms out wide to signal that everyone should be quiet and listen to him.

Pharaoh spoke loudly to the people. "Can we find anyone like this man, one in whom is the Spirit of God?"

After a short moment he spoke to Joseph so that all the people could hear. "Since God has made all this known to you, and there is no one so discerning and wise as you, you shall be in charge of my palace, and all my people are to submit to your orders. Only with respect to the throne will I be greater than you. I hereby put you in charge of the whole land of Egypt."

Then, speaking at the top of his voice so everyone would be sure to hear, Pharaoh said to Joseph, "I am Pharaoh, but without your word no one will lift hand or foot in all Egypt." Genesis 41:44 NIV

There came an astonishing outburst of cheering. The mysterious dreams that threatened Egypt had been revealed and a savior had been found. C.H. was speechless. After all his doubting, could this be true? Had the impossible happened? How could he have ever doubted the power of God? Totally enthralled, he joined the cheering and applauding.

When all was quiet Pharaoh continued. "No more shall you be called Joseph. Your name is now Zaphenath-Paaneah."

There were more cheers, and Pharaoh began to enjoy the celebration. Both he and the people realized that this was a great moment. It was the coronation of a powerful ruler.

"You are second to me in all of Egypt, and you shall attend the affairs of my government. Your word will be powerful, and my people will go out and come in by your word," declared Pharaoh.

Pharaoh spoke to Joseph, giving directions for his high-ranking officers. "From your hand will my servants and officers receive their salaries when they bow before you each month. Only in my throne will I be greater than you."

The sound of choking and coughing came from a group of officers. C.H., who was hanging on every word, jerked his head around to see who was choking. It was Potiphar.

Pharaoh took his signet ring from his finger and placed it on Joseph's finger.

Oh, where's Phygsis? wondered C.H. *He should be seeing this. That's the ring he made for the king. And now it belongs to Joseph.*

The king took the golden necklace from around his neck and placed it on Joseph. Then he put a golden crown on his head. He ordered the palace stewards to bring fine clothing for Joseph.

Great preparation got under way for all of Egypt to begin days of celebration. There was great excited activity throughout the palace. With Phygsis gone, C.H. was very busy.

The king ordered his servants to bring a special chariot and a prized horse for Joseph to ride through all the streets of the land. The regal chariot indicated authority second only to the king.

That's a beautiful horse, thought C.H. *I bet it's Lipizzaner's grandfather.*

The king organized special events. All those who played timbrels, harps, or other musical instruments were called to join in a parade. One thousand timbrels, one thousand mecholoth, and one thousand nebalim joined five thousand men with drawn swords flashing in the sunlight.

Twenty thousand of the king's finest men, outfitted in leather girdles that were ornamented with gold, marched at Joseph's right hand in a grand procession.

Joseph, regaled in his new attire and riding his chariot, passed among the throngs of people. Runners ran ahead of Joseph and yelled to the people, "Bow the knee! Bow the knee!"

Other runners ran ahead of Joseph and perfumed the road with frankincense and cassia. They scattered myrrh and aloes along the road.

Callers were positioned along the road to call out in loud voices that Joseph was chosen to be second in command in all of Egypt, and any who transgressed his orders or failed to bow the knee would die as a rebel.

There was much celebrating, and all of Egypt bowed down along the roads where Joseph traveled.

"I knew it," C.H. yelled, jumping up and down and thrusting his clenched fists into the air. The Bible story about Joseph was true!

He quickly found a private place to pray and fell to his knees. He thanked God for all that had happened.

C.H. was a changed person. With his own eyes he had seen the impossible happen. The coronation of Joseph was overwhelming proof that God's hand was active in Egypt.

"I know some clergy who need to see what I've seen," he said. "They're skeptics, purveyors of wobbly faith, and I have been fool enough to buy into their muck."

He stood and raised his arms high in the air and called out at the top of his voice, "I want to live forever! I want to live forever!" He continued this until he was exhausted and hoarse.

C.H. knelt again and continued his prayer quietly. "All things are possible with You, God. You can do anything. I have seen with my own eyes that Your hand is powerful in Egypt. You have done this thing. You made Joseph the ruler of Egypt. I must admit, I was wrong about the kid. He is a handsome dude, and he will make a great governor."

He paused for a moment, then whispered, "But I still have a problem. I need to talk to Help- —"

Before he could finish his request, the angel suddenly appeared. "Now you have seen with your own eyes, and you believe."

C.H. jumped to his feet. "You always surprise me. But I'm glad you're here. I have some questions."

"What could you question? Did you not see with your own eyes and hear with your own ears the celebration of the new governor?"

"Yes," said C.H. "But you said the stories of Joseph and Jesus are parallel, and I'm trying to understand…you know…the big picture."

"How can I help?"

"Well, I know God made it happen, and Joseph became governor of Egypt. But where is the parallel?"

"That is a good question," said the angel. "First of all, you need to hear the word of the Lord, who said, 'Remember the former things, those of long ago; I am God, and there is no other; I am God, and there is none like me. I make known the end from the beginning, from ancient times, what is still to come. I say: My purpose will stand, and I will do all that I please. From the east I summon a bird of prey; from a far-off land, a man to fulfill my purpose. What I have said, that will I bring about; what I have planned, that will I do.'" Isaiah 46:9-11 NIV

C.H. stood in silent bewilderment.

"You are now an eye witness of the former things, those of long ago. You have seen how God makes known the end from the beginning, from ancient times, what is still to come. You have witnessed how God called a man from a far country, Canaan, to come here and fight against a famine that is to be caused by an east wind. Are you with me so far?"

"So far," said C.H.

"Now, God has also called another Man, Jesus, from a far country, Canaan, to fulfill His purpose and fight against a ravenous bird of prey from the east."

As the light dawned in his head, C.H. said, "Yeah, I get it. Jesus was called from a far country, Canaan. And He is fighting a different kind of famine."

CHAPTER 14

Joseph's Family Parallels Christ's Church

I never believed it could happen," muttered C.H. to himself, thinking back to the time when he listened to seventeen-year-old Joseph's dream. "He sounded like a silly kid with fantasies of grandeur."

But now, as he watched the celebration, he was a true believer. He accepted the truth that God had made it happen. Joseph's dream had come true, and at thirty years old, he really did become governor of Egypt.

"Now, if God made Joseph's first dream come true," C.H. argued with himself, "against the odds of all this crazy Egyptian stuff, I guarantee He made the second dream happen big time! You can bet the farm on it."

C.H. watched the handsome new governor with a sense of pride as Joseph rode in the royal chariot, led by the strong horse, and passed throughout the land of Egypt.

Pharaoh's servants and officers left no stone unturned. They showed Joseph the whole land of Egypt and all the king's treasures.

Joseph appraised his situation, taking notice of his exalted situation. He lifted his eyes to heaven and said, "He raises the poor man from the dust, He lifts up the needy from the dunghill. O Lord of Host, how happy is the man who trusts in You."

After an extensive tour to familiarize himself with all the land of Egypt, Joseph returned and came before Pharaoh. The king wanted to honor him, and he arranged a special event in Joseph's honor. It was a gala affair of food, drink and celebration, and all the important people in Egypt were invited.

Egypt's best entertainers performed, and special foods were prepared and served to Joseph who sat at a table of honor.

"Bring the gifts," said Tutmosis.

A servant brought a scroll and gave it to the king. The king signed the scroll, and the servant placed it before Joseph. "You are the owner of lands, fields and vineyards," said the king.

Other servants brought sacks and chests and placed them before Joseph. "You are the owner of three thousand talents of silver, one thousand talents of gold, and one thousand talents of onyx," said the king.

One hundred men and women came in and stood before Joseph. Pharaoh said, "These are your servants. These slaves will stand before you and serve all your needs."

Joseph was greatly exalted among all the officers and noble people of Egypt.

"Your name is Zaphenath-Paaneah, and now, I command that every person in Egypt bring a gift to honor him who has a new name."

Joseph was called Zaphenath-Paaneah, the meaning of which is still being debated today.

Some believe the name means "the one who furnishes the nourishment of life."

Others believe it means "God spoke, and he came into life."

Still others believe it means "he who reveals that which is hidden."

Each belief puts forth reasonable cause to justify the interpretation. What is interesting is that all three meanings perfectly fit both Joseph and Jesus.

Pharaoh also gave Joseph a wife. He chose Asenath to be Joseph's wife.

"Joseph had no choice," C.H. mused. "The king told him who his wife would be, and that was final. I wonder why he did that."

This is fascinating, thought C.H. *I received no silver or gold, but the king said I could choose any woman in his palace…except for Nefrure, of course. But Joseph had no choice.*

The damsel Asenath was a comely virgin, and Joseph took her for a wife. The name Asenath means "belongs to," and it implies that she belonged to Joseph in body, mind, and spirit.

She was the daughter of Potiphera, the priest of Heliopolis, who was the son of Ahiram, priest of On. Heliopolis was one of the most important cities of ancient Egypt, and it was the home of the Heliopolitan theology. The sun god, Atum-Re, was the chief deity of the Heliopolitan theology.

For Asenath to totally belong to Joseph in the way that her name implied, she would need to abandon her father's Heliopolitan beliefs and share a common faith with Joseph in the one true God. Asenath became one with Joseph.

When Tutmosis gave him his new bride, he said to Joseph, "I am Pharaoh, and in all of Egypt no one shall dare to lift his hand or his foot to regulate my people without your word."

Joseph accepted the one hundred servants given to him by the king, and he purchased many more to remain in his house and to serve him.

He selected a special place in the court before the king's palace, and with the help of his many servants he built a magnificent house that was truly fit for a king. The beautiful house took three years to build. It had a temple and a special throne upon which Joseph sat.

As time passed Joseph had two sons by Asenath. The firstborn was named Manasseh, which means "God has made me forget my hardship and all of my father's house." The meaning of Manasseh's name prophesies about the Jews.

The second son was named Ephraim, which means "God has made me fruitful in the land of my misfortunes." Ephraim's name prophesies about the Gentiles.

The brothers were, of course, half Jew and half Egyptian, and herein lies an exciting clue to God's great signs.

Jesus has a bride that was chosen by God; His bride is the church. The offspring of the church are both Jew and Gentile.

Joseph had a bride who was chosen by Pharaoh: Asenath. The offspring of Asenath were both Jew and Egyptian.

C.H. was struggling to comprehend all that had happened and trying hard to remember his goal of finding points of congruency.

Actually, I don't care about points anymore. I just want the Bread of Heaven. I want to live forever, he thought. Nevertheless, he kept searching for God's great signs.

C.H. took a lonely stroll and found a large, flat stone on which to sit. He sat with his elbows on his knees and his face in his hands in deep thought.

"I'm a dead man, and I can't ask for the Bread of Heaven until I return to my sorry old drowned body."

He started rocking back and forth in frustration and groaning as if he were in pain. He repeated over and over, "I need the Bread. I need the Bread."

Finally he said, "I need help. God help me."

"How might I help you?" inquired the angel, suddenly appearing in front of him.

C.H. jumped to his feet. "Helper!" he cried. "You always startle me."

"How might I help you?" the angel repeated.

"I have a problem," said C.H. "I want the Bread of Heaven."

"We've already discussed that. Dead men may not ask for the Bread of Heaven. It is too late."

"I know," said C.H. "But I have another problem."

The angel waited.

C.H. paused, recalling an earlier conversation he'd had with the angel. Finally, he stated his problem. "You once said that the power structure in Egypt during Joseph's reign as governor foresees and parallels the power structure in heaven."

"Yes, I said that," said the angel. "It is God's symbolism."

"Well, you were wrong," snorted C.H.

"Wrong?"

"Yes. See, I've been thinking. The power structure in heaven is the Trinity, right? God in three persons. I've heard it preached a thousand times. I've even sung about it. Everybody in the world knows about the Trinity. But I'm telling you, there is not a hint of a shadow of a third person in the power structure in Egypt."

C.H. clasped his hands behind him and walked a few feet away from the angel. He turned and thrust his hands toward the angel. With emotion he said, "I was at Joseph's grand party, and I saw all the great people of Egypt. There is no one in Egypt who can so much as spit without Joseph's approval. Face it, you were wrong. So now I want to forget about this whole congruency scheme."

"You may stop your search if you wish," replied the angel.

"Fat chance. I'm here to stay, and I'm going to find the bread. But I'm through with this parallel stuff.

"Very well," said the angel.

"Do you see my problem?" asked C.H. with tears glistening in his eyes. "And that's not all. I have another problem."

"May I hear what it is?"

"I'm looking for other points of congruency, and I'm not finding them. For example, Joseph has two sons. But Jesus didn't have any children. How can Joseph model Jesus?"

"Do you not remember that Jacob, who is called Israel, came to Egypt?" the angel said. "And there Israel met his grandsons, Manasseh and Ephraim. Israel took Manasseh and Ephraim away from Joseph and told Joseph that they were no longer his sons."

"I guess I had forgotten that part of the story," C.H. mumbled.

"Joseph's father told him that he had no children, and that Manasseh and Ephraim, the offspring of Asenath, were now his brothers. Israel told Joseph that Manasseh and Ephraim would receive their inheritance from him, Israel, because they were his sons and he was their father."

"That's really strange."

The angel continued. "Consider carefully. Scripture speaks of the bride of Christ. Are you aware that the church is Jesus' bride?"

"Yeah, I've heard that."

"Jesus is the Savior of both Jews and Gentiles. They are the offspring of His bride, the church. But neither Jew nor Gentile will receive their inheritance from Jesus. No, they will receive their inheritance from God the Father."

"That's amazing," said C.H. "The stories really are parallel."

CHAPTER 15

The Bread of Egypt

C.H. stood at the bottom of one of the large, deep chambers located just outside the south wall of the Step Pyramid complex. All the huge pits were connected by underground tunnels. Surely, there was genius in the design.

All the grain that was stored in the chambers could be accessed from the main pit, which had a long staircase from the bottom of the pit to the complex wall.

This sucker is big, thought C.H. *You could put an ocean of grain in these chambers.*

Considerable work and cleaning had been done to make the huge complex ready to receive grain. Other storage facilities had been built in most of the cities of Egypt, but the one at Sakkara was by far the largest. It was lined with white limestone from nearby Mukattam Hills, and the walls rose several feet above ground level, giving all eleven chambers greater capacity.

Now, for the first time, some grain was being brought in for storage in the great facility, and C.H. watched the workers.

Joseph had appointed officers and commissioners throughout Egypt to oversee the harvesting and to operate the storage facilities in the cities.

C.H. recalled Joseph's words to Pharaoh: "Let Pharaoh look for a wise man and put him in charge of the land of Egypt." Joseph also told Pharaoh to appoint commissioners over the land to take a fifth of the harvest of Egypt during the seven years of abundance.

Joseph said, "And now let Pharaoh look for a discerning and wise man and put him in charge of the land of Egypt. Let Pharaoh appoint commissioners over the land to take a fifth of the harvest of Egypt during the seven years of abundance. They should collect all the food of these good years that are coming and store up the grain under the authority of Pharaoh, to be kept in the cities for food. This food should be held in reserve for the country, to be used during the seven years of famine that will come upon Egypt, so that the country may not be ruined by the famine." Genesis 41:33-36 NIV

Now this had all been done and the actual harvesting and storing had begun.

God gave Joseph wisdom, and he was proving himself to be a wise and powerful vizier of Egypt. He was implementing his God-given plan. Not only had Joseph gained authority over the land of Egypt, but he had gone out into all the land in a vigilant effort to implement a monumental task that involved the entire land of Egypt.

God is not an impulse designer. Eight and a half centuries before Joseph became governor of Egypt, God's signs were already shaping the story that would reveal the secret of long ages past. The designer of the amazing set of huge chambers had no clue that his work on the ancient monument was also the work of God.

Sakkara is the location of the Step Pyramid, the first pyramid ever built, and it lies on the west bank of the Nile just north of Memphis. It is part of the great necropolis of Memphis.

The first pyramid was built as much as eight hundred years prior to Joseph's reign in Egypt, and it was built for the eternal glory of King Netjerykhet Djoser. It was designed and built by the genius builder Imhotep, who was then Egypt's vizier, and who was worshipped by the Egyptians as a god.

The pyramid was placed in a beautiful and elaborate complex with a wall around it, and Joseph had the entire complex restored and made ready to serve as a center of commerce.

Before descending into the huge pit, C.H. entered the complex at the main entrance on the south end of the east wall. He strolled along the colonnade, where two rows of columns formed a passageway from the entrance to an area along the south wall that led to the enormous pits.

There were twenty columns on each side of the passage, and each column formed the end of another wall that reached back perpendicular to the main walls. All together, the columns formed forty separate rooms or booth areas. A wide, straight passage passed between the rooms and ran the entire length of the colonnade, from the entrance on the east to the west end near the huge pits.

C.H. climbed the elaborate stairway and made his way back to the colonnade. With his hands clasped behind his back, he strolled along the colonnade, counting the three-sided rooms.

His search for the Bread of Heaven had filled him with curiosity and questions about all things Egyptian. He was truly a reporter in hot pursuit of a story.

He counted twenty rooms along each side, and they had all been made ready for use as sales booths. While no grain was to be sold for seven years, many farmers would be visiting the Step Pyramid complex, bringing grain for storage. It was apparent that Joseph was implementing his plan quite well.

"Reminds me of a farmer's market," C.H. said to himself.

C.H. was becoming experienced in Egyptian ways while working in the king's food service. Nefrure demanded that he not live in the palace without surgery, and he had maneuvered himself into a kitchen crew that lived and worked in the Step Pyramid complex.

"Here's where the action will be," he said to himself. He had learned the ancient art of Egyptian brewing and had become the brewmaster in the complex.

Bread and beer were the two staples most common in the Egyptian farmers' diet. Joseph wanted the farmers to be treated as guests when they brought their crops to storage.

C.H. made beer by starting with a sprouted mix of wheat and barley. He cooked it lightly to add flavor and to release its sugar. To this mix he added just the right amount of water and sometimes some more grains with yeast. Natural fermentation would begin, and in due process he ended up with a strong, nutritious beer.

Beer in ancient Egypt served two useful purposes. It was an excellent source of nutrition and calories. And it was safer to drink than most of the water.

C.H. found a place where he could view the grain that was being brought from the fields and stored in the large chambers. The carts and donkeys were coming more frequently, and C.H. could see many carts in the distance coming from different directions. Farmers with black makeup on their eyes and naked upper bodies delivered their grain to the granary.

This complex is like a small city, thought C.H. *And those pits will hold a lot of grain. Lots of it is going to be stored today alone.*

He looked at the huge chambers, which were covered with wooden roofs. Joseph was planning to store enough grain under those roofs to feed the world for seven years. C.H. tried to comprehend the enormity of Joseph's plan.

"Here I am, searching for the Bread of Heaven, but all I'm seeing is the bread of Egypt. You know, I'd give ten-to-one odds this whole grain story symbolizes the Bread of Heaven."

Outside the walls of the Step Pyramid complex, a short distance away, was a stable and a fenced area for donkeys, horses, camels, and pack mules. Visitors found it useful for tending their animals for the time they were at the complex.

"Points, symbolism, and parallels?" pondered C.H. "Where in the heavenly realm is all this grain pointing?"

"The amount of grain they could put in those big chambers and in all the storage facilities in the other cities is…" He scratched his head. "Beyond measure," he said, answering his own question.

"When the famine comes, grain is going to save the lives of everyone in Egypt. Heck, people will come from all over the world to buy this grain."

C.H. walked around, pulling at his chin and thinking. "There are some profound things going on here," he said to himself. "A jealous Egyptian Pharaoh with absolute power has come from a long line of Pharaohs, reaching back from antiquity, all ingrained with an insatiable desire for power and glory. Yet he has willingly stepped aside and handed sweeping power to a young man from a faraway country."

He walked and talked to himself, occasionally checking in to see how the brewing was going. He and his staff were becoming popular with the Egyptian farmers who enjoyed some refreshment after they deposited their grain.

"How could this happen?" C.H. asked. "I mean, the king hated Hatshepsut for grabbing his power. Yet there are no limits to Joseph's authority, except Pharaoh himself."

C.H. froze as he pursued his thought. Sudden fear clutched at him. *What if…No, he would never do it. But it would be a piece of cake for Joseph to overthrow the throne and take complete control.*

The thought made C.H. weak kneed. He sat down.

That's incredible, he thought. He also thought it was incredible that Joseph did not consider equality with Pharaoh as something to be grabbed.

"Hey, there's one more way he models Christ."

CHAPTER 16

Egyptian Farmers

Egyptian farmland is among the most extraordinary in the world. In the days of Joseph, Egypt was a country of agriculture, and the majority of the people in the country were farmers. The rest of society lived off the labors and the harvests of the brown-bodied field workers.

A narrow strip of fertile valley follows the longest river in the world, the Nile, from the wide expanse of the African Sahara in the south to the Delta that spills into the Mediterranean in the north. The west bank is referred to as the Libyan, and the east bank is referred to as the Arabian. Beyond the fertile valley in both directions is a barren desert called the "red earth," where caravans travel and burial sites are constructed.

Neither fertilizer nor crop rotation has ever been needed in Egypt. The annual inundation that comes during the rainy season in Upper Egypt brings moisture and nutrients to the elongated, fertile valley. A layer of fresh black silt is laid down over the entire farming area of Egypt each year.

The watershed that feeds the 4,240-mile-long Nile River comes from monsoonal downpours as far south as the mountains surrounding the area of Lake Victoria. Water flows into the surging White Nile, which flows northward through central Africa and joins a confluence with the

Blue Nile that drains from the great Ethiopian plain. From there the Nile courses thousands of miles north to a place where it slows and spreads over the vast delta area.

Not everything was perfect for the Egyptian farmer, however. He had plenty of enemies, including mice, rats, birds, worms, locusts, cattle, hippopotami, and, worst of all, tax collectors.

The Egyptian farmers had many gods to help them in their struggles. Khnum, god of the First Cataract, received the credit for keeping the great Nile valley safe and making matters punctual and orderly.

The calendar was very important to the Egyptians. They were one of the first people in the world to have a calendar. They watched each year for the arrival of the huge flock of white birds called ibises to come from the south, indicating that it was time for the waters to start rising. The ibises were the embodiment of the god Thoth.

Osiris was the god of all things moist and green and growing, and grain symbolized his body. But alas, he met misfortune when his evil brother killed him.

As the unsprouted grain lay prone through a season, so would Osiris. Fortunately, Osiris' wife (who was also his sister) was also a god. Her name was Isis. She made the grain sprout and grow, and thereby brought her husband back to life for a happy season each year.

The evil brother who killed Osiris was Seth, the devil god who ruled the red land with scorching heat and devastating winds. Seth could kill men and their animals, ruin crops, and bring great destruction.

The Hermaphrodite god Hapy was a man with large female breasts. It was his job to make the inundation match the irrigation needs of the farmer. Egyptian farmers had a god for almost every need.

The Egyptians considered Joseph to be a strange man. He was honest and just and kind and forthright, yet he was a firm ruler who demanded compliance. The strangest thing about Joseph was his faith in only one God. He claimed that his God was God over all things.

Whatever Joseph tried to do, he first appealed to his one God, and his God made all things work well. Joseph was successful. He assembled a large work force of commissioners and created a work ethic and a spirit of unity.

The first annual crop of grain under Joseph's rule was so abundant that Joseph became an immediate national hero. It was spectacular that Joseph's God could do such things.

The Egyptians were filled with awe. The crops were the most abundant the Egyptians had ever seen. Harvests went well, and Egypt's granaries became filled to overflowing.

Unlike the tax collectors, who had gone out to the farmers and carried away large portions of the crop, Joseph asked each farmer to bring one fifth of his extraordinary harvest to the granary.

He organized a large number of commissioners to teach standard practices to the farmers and to oversee them and help them be successful. They were taught how to harvest, thresh, and bag the grain before bringing it to the granary. They were told to set aside seed grain for the following year.

Grain Sales

Commissioners were assigned to keep a record of the grain that was stored in all the granaries in the land of Egypt. The grain continued to come in abundance. When all the granaries in the land were filled to overflowing, it became impossible to keep count of it all.

Finally, the effort to measure was abandoned, and it became sufficient to say that the amount of grain stored in Egypt was beyond measure.

C.H. marveled at the grain as it came to the big granary. He stood with his hands on his hips and shook his head.

This would make a heck of a story to write, he thought. *I can see the headline: "Joseph Becomes Governor of Egypt." Or how about "Grain Beyond Measure"? Yeah, that's better. The grain should get the headline because we're talking life and death for a lot of people here.*

Besides the abundant cultivated crops of grain that grew in Egypt during the seven years of bounty, there were many other things that grew. Some grew wild, such as shrubs, herbs, acacias, tamarisks, mimosas, willows, palms, dates, and lemon trees. Even humble houses had small gardens with vegetables and flowers. Grapes were found in most gardens, and simple winemaking routines were commonplace.

There were dense growths of papyrus throughout the delta area of the Nile in what is now called Lower Egypt.

For seven years the Nile valley was a lush place, and the people who lived there ate very well.

C.H. watched the Step Pyramid complex become an important center of commerce. News of the enormous supply of grain became widespread all around the world.

But after seven years, things changed. It was no surprise to anyone when the next part of Pharaoh's dream became reality. Bad times came abruptly in the eighth year. The monsoonal rains in central Africa were light, and the water in the Nile diminished. The inundation was almost nonexistent, and natural growth became parched. An east wind blew and dried out the land.

Egyptian gardens were parched, and crops did not produce. Wildlife suffered, and hunting and fishing was scarce. The famine was upon Egypt and all the face of the earth.

Farmers who had laid up grain for themselves, but not according to Joseph's instructions, opened their storehouses and found that all the food in their stores was full of vermin and not fit to eat. This created great alarm as the harsh famine prevailed throughout the land.

Starving Egyptians began to cry out in hunger. Some went to Pharaoh and asked for food, and Pharaoh told them to go to Joseph. There were no exceptions. Joseph was the only one who could give them food.

"Go to Joseph," Pharaoh said, "and do whatever he tells you."

"Helper was right. It's discrimination! What we have here is the bread of Egypt," C.H. mused. "And you don't have a choice. You've got to have it or you're dead. But there is only one source: Joseph. So, where's the parallel in heaven?"

Joseph opened the warehouses, and sales of grain began. The Step Pyramid complex became a beehive of activity. Joseph had to establish his own office in the complex because no one was allowed to buy grain without his approval.

The forty rooms in the colonnade were activated as sales booths, and each booth had specially trained people ready to do business. Interpreters were on hand to help buyers from other countries.

C.H. learned the hieroglyphics for numbers. He learned that:

a tally, or slash mark (/), equals one,
a heel bone equals ten,
a coil of rope equals one hundred,
a lotus flower equals one thousand,
a bent stick equals ten thousand,
a fish equals one hundred thousand,
and an astonished man equals one million.

He also learned that the Egyptians wrote numbers from left to right in ascending order. For example, the number 105 would be written /////9. First would come five tallies, or slash marks. Since each tally represents one, five of them would equal five. This would be followed by a coil of rope (which looked very much like the numeral 9). The coil of rope equals 100. Thus, 105 would appear as /////9.

As the months of hardship wore on, more and more Egyptians came to buy grain. The complex at Sakkara was busy every day. The people came not only to buy grain, but also to take advantage of Joseph's hospitality and enjoy some fresh-baked bread and freshly brewed beer while doing business at the Step Pyramid complex.

C.H. was intrigued by the sales transactions. There was no official money minted by the government, so anything that had intrinsic value was acceptable as tender.

Currencies in ancient Egypt and Canaan had much in common. So when Joseph was taken from Canaan to Egypt, he did not have much to learn about finance in his new country.

The most common currency was pieces of silver, although there were also brass and gold. Silver was usually weighed in shekels, which was about 220 grains. Shekels of silver were often made into rings.

Bekas were half shekels. A talent was about 3,000 shekels. Things like myrrh, cinnamon, fragrant cane, fine spices, cassia, and olive oil were sold by weight or quantity.

During the seven bad years in Egypt, everything of value that could be used to buy or barter grain became more precious.

CHAPTER 18

To Egypt for Grain

Envision a family tree of symbolism, and place Jacob at the top. The father of the world's most significant family was the symbolic father of both good and evil, and his family symbolized the great battle of the ages caused by the enmity between the serpent's seed and Eve's seed.

When the serpent tempted Eve in the Garden of Eden, God rebuked the serpent, and He told the serpent, "I will put enmity between you and the woman, and between your offspring and hers; he will crush your head, and you will strike his heel." Genesis 3:15 NIV

Now, every soul who lives is thrust into the midst of that enmity and must wrestle in the great battle of the ages.

Jacob symbolized this in a wrestling match. Once, he was on his way to meet his brother Esau, and he was very fearful that Esau would kill him and his family, because there was enmity between himself and his twin.

At night he took his two wives, his two maids, and his eleven children (Benjamin had not yet been born) and crossed the river at Jabbok. He returned to the other side and remained alone, and a man wrestled with him until daybreak.

When it became apparent to the man that he could not prevail against Jacob, he struck him on the hip, and Jacob's hip received a permanent injury.

The man said, "Let go; the day is breaking."

Jacob said, "No, not until you bless me."

The man asked, "What is your name?"

He said, "Jacob."

The man said, "You shall no longer be called Jacob. You are Israel. You have wrestled with God and with man, and have prevailed."

Jacob called the place where he wrestled Peniel, which means, "I have seen God face to face."

He was the father of the symbolic morning and the symbolic evening. He was the father of the symbolically bruised head and the symbolically bruised heel. He was struck on the hip, halfway between the head and the heel, and at the midpoint that symbolizes noon. In God's symbolism, injuries came to those of the symbolic noontime.

Therefore, it was with a limp that the patriarch moved among the tents of his beloved family of sixty-six. The famine had come upon Canaan, and Jacob, now called Israel, had a major problem. He must find food for a household of three generations, plus male and female servants, and his large flocks.

The famine that struck Egypt was just as severe in Canaan, and Jacob could see that he and his family were in serious trouble. The fields of Canaan gave no grain, and it became apparent that Jacob and all of his people and herds were in imminent danger of starvation.

News of grain in Egypt was being talked about throughout the whole world, and Jacob heard the news. He knew about the grain in Egypt, and he knew that foreigners from many countries were going there to purchase grain. He also learned that no one could buy grain unless they first received approval from Zaphenath-Paaneah, the exalted governor.

Jacob said to his sons, "Why stand there and look at each other? Will you rejoice when we all starve? Have you not heard that there is grain in Egypt? Go down there and buy some for us, so that we may live and not die."

Jacob's ten older sons harkened keenly to their father's voice, and they went, like many from around the world, to the land of Egypt. They rode camels, and took pack animals and grain sacks and money to pay for the grain.

But Jacob, now called Israel, would not let his youngest son, Benjamin, go. His aching heart remembered the tragedy of his beloved Joseph, and he wept daily over his great loss. He would not consider putting Benjamin in harm's way.

"When you arrive in Egypt," Jacob told his ten sons, "do not create suspicion nor upset the inhabitants. Do not enter the city as a group, but go in one at a time and pass unobserved."

His sons agreed to go as their father instructed. But they were worried because of a dark secret they had kept from their father. They'd heard that the Midianites, to whom they had sold their brother Joseph, had in turn sold him to the sons of Ishmael, who then took him to Egypt as a slave.

Now that they were headed to Egypt, their misdeeds weighed heavily on their hearts, and they became extremely repentant.

"We will find him," declared one, "and ransom him."

"If we cannot buy him fairly," said another, "we will slay his master and take him by force."

The brothers made a pact. "If we must die for him, we will," they agreed.

People from all over the world were coming to Egypt to buy grain because the famine was severe. Joseph felt sure he would see someone from his family eventually. He believed that his brothers would travel from Canaan to Egypt to buy grain. So he began to make plans.

First, he passed a law that grain could not be sold to anyone's servant. Jacob's family had servants, and Joseph did not want them to come on behalf of the family. Second, no grain could be resold; anyone caught reselling grain would be put to death. Joseph did not want wholesalers to get grain for his family. Joseph also declared that anyone caught leading two or three pack animals loaded with grain would be put to death.

Joseph put salvation on a personal basis. There would be no salvation by proxy. He wanted to make sure there was no way his brothers could buy grain without coming before him. He closed all the granaries in Egypt except the big one at Sakkara.

Joseph placed sentinels at all the gates and roads that led to Sakkara. Everyone entering had to give his name and his father's name. The names were gathered at the end of each business day and brought to Joseph that evening.

Everyone from around the world who came to buy grain complied with the statutes and regulations.

When the sons of Jacob entered the city, they did as their father had instructed them to do. They each entered separately, then regrouped inside the city to plan their search for their lost brother, Joseph.

Joseph knew immediately when and where his brothers had entered Egypt.

"Where should we search for Joseph?" asked one brother when they had regrouped.

"Such a handsome young slave would surely be sold as a prostitute," offered another.

So the brothers went to the walls of the harlots and searched for Joseph for three days. Meanwhile, Joseph's men, who had lost track of the brothers, were searching for them. Joseph's men searched all of Egypt, including Goshen and Rameses. Finally, they found them at the walls of the harlots.

C.H. enjoyed watching the strangers and foreigners come to buy grain, so he often spent his spare time in the big colonnade where business was transacted. He walked along, glancing in each of the forty sales booths that were equipped with woven rugs and tables built low to the ground, and watched the sales attendants busily selling grain.

He looked at the various kinds of payment that were being accepted in exchange for the grain. Suddenly, in one sales booth, something caught his eye. There in the mix of the various pieces of silver and other coins was a familiar piece of jewelry. It was the golden medallion he had taken from the dead body of Hatshepsut.

"Phygsis!" he cried loudly. "Phygsis has been here."

C.H. scurried about, looking for his old colleague, but there was no sign of him. He left the colonnade and walked through the crowds in the courtyard of the big plaza.

He saw Joseph's head steward standing near the entrance to the complex headquarters. Behind the steward were an army captain, thirty spear bearers, and ten ax warriors, all standing in line with their weapons thrust forward.

Seven trumpeters stood across from the steward, holding their trumpets at ready. Joseph's horses and chariot were being tended nearby. Joseph's horses were the only animals allowed inside the walls of the huge complex.

As C.H. hurried through the complex, he saw ten foreign-looking men standing before Joseph's steward. He froze in his tracks. The brothers were powerful and scary-looking men. "Oh, man! Look who's here," he said, recognizing Joseph's older brothers, whom he had seen in Canaan. "Yep, that's them all right. Reuben, Simeon, Levi, Judah, Issachar, Zebulun, Dan, Naphtali, Gad, and Asher."

C.H. was unaware that Joseph had planned the setup, but he knew this was a special moment in time. These tough, hungry-looking men had traveled far from home, looking for food to save their lives and the lives of their families.

Joseph's men had found them and brought them to this place. The fix was in, because Joseph wanted his brothers to come to his house and bow before him.

The Egyptians helped them put their pack animals in the corrals outside the complex.

"What is your purpose here?" asked the steward.

"We have come to buy grain," they answered.

"No one can buy grain without approval," replied the steward. "Do you seek the one who furnishes the nourishment of life?"

"Yes," they answered.

"Zaphenath-Paaneah rules. He is lord of Egypt's granaries," replied the steward.

The men were escorted to Joseph's house and then to the temple where Joseph was sitting on his throne. C.H. followed with the steward and his entourage.

Suddenly, the sons of Jacob stood face to face with the younger brother they had hated so much. They did not recognize him. They had not seen him for twenty years and he was no longer the kid they remembered. Instead, Joseph looked and sounded like an Egyptian governor.

Joseph sat upon his throne in the temple, clothed with princely garments. He wore a large golden crown, and he was surrounded by many mighty and important men. He spoke the Egyptian language as though it were his native tongue.

The eyes of the men from Canaan grew wide as they surveyed the powerful and comely figure. The dignity of his countenance appeared wonderful to their eyes, and they bowed down in awe to the ground before him.

Joseph's brothers were grown men when he last saw them, and while they were now twenty years older, he had no trouble recognizing them instantly. He understood their language as they spoke to one another, but he pretended not to.

Joseph called out loudly for one of his interpreters to come and assist him in speaking with these ten visitors. The brothers stayed bowed with their faces to the ground before him.

Joseph looked at his brothers and, for a split second, he had a flashback of a dream. He saw himself and his brothers binding sheaves in the field. Then his sheaf rose and stood upright, and his brothers' sheaves gathered around his and bowed down to it.

Then Joseph heard an echo that had bounced around in his head for two decades. He recalled the time he was in a pit like a captured animal, and he was looking up into the faces of strangers who lifted him from the pit. He recalled how the strangers had a confrontation with his brothers.

Finally, the strangers had asked the ransom price for the rescued kid, and Joseph heard the price. The words came back: "twenty shekels of silver."

Joseph blinked the moisture from his eyes, cleared his throat, and asked, "Where do you come from?"

"From the land of Canaan," they replied. "To buy food."

When C.H. realized that the brothers, who had hated Joseph so much, did not now recognize him, he exhaled a great sigh of relief. "Oh, baby! Let's have no rough stuff, now," he whispered to himself.

Joseph spoke harshly to his brothers. "You are spies! You have come to see the nakedness of Egypt."

"No, my lord," Simeon quickly pleaded.

"Your servants have come to buy food," said Levi. "We are all the sons of one man. Your servants are honest men, not spies."

"Come now," Joseph said. "If you have come to Egypt to purchase grain as you say, why have you separated yourselves to enter through ten different gates of the city? That is the way of spies."

"They are liars and murderers," C.H. muttered to himself.

He remembered a story about Simeon and Levi that had burned an impression in his mind. When Jacob's family was camped near the city of Shechem, their sister Dinah was raped by Shechem, son of Hamor, who wanted her for a wife.

Jacob's sons deceived the men of Shechem by telling them that they could marry their women if they would all agree to be circumcised. The men of Shechem agreed, and three days later, when the pain was most severe, Simeon and Levi took their swords and killed every male in the city.

Even Reuben, who tried to save Joseph, was no angel. C.H. recalled that he was the one who took Bilhah, Jacob's concubine, to bed. "They are no good!" he whispered to himself.

As C.H. thought about their treachery, he looked at the strong postures of the sons of Jacob and shook his head in awe.

"It is not true, my lord," Judah said. "We are not spies. We are all brothers, the sons of one man who lives in Canaan. Our father commanded us to enter the city in a way to avoid trouble."

"How can they stand there and call themselves servants and say they are honest?" C.H. mumbled.

"I do not believe you," Joseph said sternly to his brothers. "You have come to see where our land is unprotected."

"Your servants were twelve brothers," Reuben said meekly. "I am the eldest. Our father is Jacob, the son of Isaac, the son of Abraham, the Hebrew. Our youngest brother is now with our father, and one is no more because he was lost in Egypt. He may be a slave. We are seeking him throughout the land, even in the houses of the harlots because of his youth and comeliness."

"If you find your brother in the land of Egypt, and his master will not part with him for a great price, what will you do?" asked Joseph.

"We will slay the man, take our brother, and bring him home," Simeon replied. The other brothers agreed.

"You have come to avenge your brother," said Joseph, "the same way you avenged your sister when you smote all the inhabitants of Shechem."

"No," said Judah. "We have come to buy grain."

"Your disguise does not work. Surely you speak falsely and utter lies. You are spies! And this is how you will be tested: As surely as Pharaoh lives, you will not leave this place unless your youngest brother comes here."

There was a long pause. A recurring sound came to C.H.'s ears. It was the sound of a woman weeping softly. The sound went away as quickly as it came.

Finally, Joseph said, "Let one of you go and bring your brother, while the rest of you remain here. Your words will be tested, whether there is truth in you. If not, as Pharaoh lives, surely you are spies."

Joseph waited, but there was no response from the brothers. After a moment Joseph held his hands out wide. "What is your answer?"

There was still no response, so Joseph spoke to his army captain, who stood with a troop of mighty men. The ten brothers were arrested and marched off to prison.

Three days later, as C.H. was walking through the busy compound, he saw Joseph, with his brothers standing before him. He had ordered his brothers to be brought before him to once again demand that the younger brother, Benjamin, be brought to Egypt. Ten spear bearers stood behind the brothers, and ten archers stood on each side. Twenty more stood behind Joseph.

The interpreter was there, and Joseph was talking through him. He said, "Do this and you will live, for I fear God. If you are honest men, let one of your brothers stay here. The rest of you shall go and carry grain back to Canaan that your family might have food. But this thing you must do: bring your youngest brother here to me. When you do that, your words will prove to be true, and you shall not die."

The brothers talked among themselves. Finally they agreed to do what Joseph had demanded.

Joseph heard the brothers speak of their guilt. He heard them say that they were paying the penalty for what they had done to him. They remembered the pain and the fear they saw in their younger brother's eyes when he pleaded with them. They agreed that the trouble they now had was because of what they had done.

Reuben said, "I told you not to harm the boy, but you would not listen. Now you are paying for your misdeeds. His blood in on your hands."

C.H. walked around to a position some distance behind Joseph where he could see the brothers' faces. When the men spoke of their remorse and how sad they were over the wrong they had committed against their younger brother, Joseph turned away from them and took a few steps to put some distance between himself and his brothers.

C.H. could see tears in Joseph's eyes.

A few minutes passed. Finally Joseph turned back and spoke to the army captain. Soldiers grabbed Simeon and bound his hands behind him. The other brothers watched as Simeon, his feet bound so tightly he could take only small steps, was taken to prison.

When Simeon was removed from the sight of his brothers, Joseph sent a runner to bring the steward of his own house. He sent another runner to the colonnade to summon the manager of grain sales to come and receive some instructions about selling grain to the men from Canaan.

When the steward and the sales attendant came, Joseph spoke to them in Egyptian, without an interpreter, so his brothers could not understand what he was saying. He told them to sell the men as much grain as they wished to buy.

He then told them to do a strange thing. He said, "When you have received their money in payment for the grain they are buying, tell them you will load their donkeys and make them ready for the trip home. Divert them with beer and bread and give them sustenance for the journey."

Joseph lowered his voice and spoke privately to his steward. "While they are diverted, you are to secrete each man's money back into his grain sack. Each man is to receive all the money back that he paid to purchase the grain. See to it that they do not know what you have done."

Joseph continued. "Bind the sacks securely so they cannot learn what has been done until they are well departed, when they open their sacks."

Leaving Simeon behind, the brothers headed home. They were apprehensive about what they had agreed to do and wondered how they could explain matters to their father, Jacob.

"We did not find our brother Joseph," said one brother, "and our father will be in great pain to learn that we must bring his beloved son before the great ruler."

"The man is very hard," said another. "What could we do? He accused us of being spies."

After a day's journey toward home, they arrived at an inn. As they prepared to spend the night there, Reuben decided to tend the donkeys. "I will open one of the sacks of grain," he said, "to give the animals some provender."

The brothers were resting and discussing their trip when Reuben returned. He approached them holding something in his hands, a look of confusion on his face. He could say nothing.

"Look, Reuben has returned," said Gad. "Does he have a problem?"

"Something has stolen his breath," said Levi.

Reuben simply held out his hands to show what he was carrying. It was a handful of money.

The brothers jumped to their feet to look at the money.

"This is the same money I used to pay for my sack," he said. "When this is discovered, we will all be in prison with Simeon."

Confused and frightened, they agreed to go home and explain all that happened to their father.

Jacob listened to his sons recount all the strange events of their trip to Egypt. He fell into a sickness and lay upon his bed. His sons gathered around and continued to explain matters to their father. But nothing could comfort Jacob.

Reuben's money being returned to his sack sounded very strange to Jacob. He said, "Look in your other sacks."

The brothers all checked their sacks and were astounded to find the money in the mouths of every sack. The very same money they had used to pay for the grain.

Jacob's heart was broken when he learned that Simeon was being held prisoner. He was even more pained when he learned that Zaphen-ath-Paaneah demanded that Benjamin must be brought before him.

"My sons are being taken away from me," he said. "Joseph is gone, Simeon is gone. You may not take Benjamin from me."

Days passed and circumstances prevailed. The famine was severe in all the world, and in Canaan there was no food. The grain purchased from Egypt was running short, and life-and-death matters arose again.

Jacob told his sons to go back to Egypt to buy grain, yet he refused to consider the demand that Benjamin go with them. His sons argued with him.

"The man will not release Simeon," Judah said, "nor sell us grain if we disobey his demand to bring our younger brother."

A heartbroken, frustrated Jacob discussed the matter with his sons, but he would not agree to send Benjamin.

Reuben said, "You may kill my two sons if I do not bring him back to you."

All the brothers came around their father and made similar persuasions. They offered their wives and their children. But Israel would not relent. He would not agree to let Benjamin go. He said, "My son shall not go down with you, for his brother is dead, and he alone is left. If harm should come to him on the journey, it would bring down my gray hairs with sorrow to Sheol."

CHAPTER 19

I Choose You, I Choose You

In his spare time C.H. loved to take walks and meditate. The angel had told him to think carefully about the many things he would see in Egypt. He often reminded himself that he was searching for points of congruency while pursuing the Bread of Heaven.

God had granted him, a dead man, the privilege to search for the Bread of Heaven by observing the great signs in Egypt that reveal the secrets of long ages past. Hopefully, the parallels between the story of Joseph and the story of Jesus would lead him to the Bread of Heaven.

Being the brewmaster was easy. The job mostly entailed delegating responsibility to a trained staff. So C.H. had plenty of time to walk around and think. He had a habit of walking slowly with his hands clasped behind him, talking quietly to himself.

The colonnade was full of people buying grain, and there was the usual hustle and bustle of bringing grain from the big granary and helping customers load their pack animals or carts.

C.H. walked the length of the colonnade and exited through the entrance of the complex. The entrance was on the south end of the east wall, and beyond the entrance outside the complex was a crowd of people who had bought grain and were trying to get it loaded to leave for their homes. Some customers were arriving, and they were tethering their animals and preparing to enter the colonnade to purchase grain.

C.H. walked and talked to himself. "Grain, grain, grain. Man, there is a lot of grain in this place. I'm sure now that grain must symbolize the Bread of Heaven."

As he looked around at the people, he had great pity for them. The famine was devastating. "Look at all these starving people," he muttered to himself. "They've got to have grain or it's good-bye, baby."

C.H. saw a woman standing near her bag of grain. A head covering obscured her face. As he strolled past her, she turned slightly to keep her back toward him.

C.H. remained deep in thought, trying to sort out all the possible points of congruency that the story in ancient Egypt reflected in matters surrounding the story of Jesus.

"Bet they come back," he muttered. "Joseph's eleven brothers symbolize Jesus' apostles. There were eleven of them, not counting Judas, who betrayed Him. Their eyes were not fully open to know their brother, who was also their Savior."

He stopped and looked about. The woman standing near her bag of grain still had her back toward him.

He continued walking and talking to himself. "Joseph spoke to his brothers through an interpreter. Jesus spoke to his disciples in parables. That could mean something."

He stopped again and held out his hands as if he were explaining a tough situation to his editor. "Joseph held his brothers hostage for three days. Hmm. Jesus spent three days in the tomb. Maybe he held somebody's faith hostage. That could mean something too."

C.H. continued his line of thinking. "OK, one brother got no grain because he was in jail. What does that mean? Maybe Judas, who got no Bread from Heaven?" He shook his head. "Beats me. Maybe when the brothers come back the second time, they'll symbolize something else."

After a few minutes of kicking around his ideas, he slapped his forehead with his open palm. "That's it! They will come again. It will be like the resurrection. He will not be dead, and their minds will be opened, and they will recognize him."

C.H. looked up toward heaven. "The best deal of all is that their money was put back in their sacks. You know why? Because the Bread of Heaven is free."

He thought of Helper's advice. "I must learn to read God's signs."

He took a few more slow steps with his hands clasped behind him. "Drat! Some of this stuff works and some doesn't. Where's the Trinity? We have a father and a beloved son and some brothers. Symbolically we have a problem."

C.H. decided to head back to the Step Pyramid complex. As he drew near the entrance, he noticed the same woman standing by her sack of grain. The woman had apparently stood by her sack of grain all day.

Poor little gal, he thought. *Maybe I should check this out.*

As C.H. approached the woman, she turned slightly to keep her back toward him. When he got quite close, he thought he recognized her. She looked like the tattooed dancer from Pharaoh's palace. But she was thin and had the same hungry look so common among the many starving Egyptians.

"Isis," he said, "is that you?"

The woman dropped to her knees and started crying.

C.H. stood quietly for a minute, then said, "Isis, you obviously have a problem. Do you want to tell me about it?"

Finally, Isis stopped crying enough to speak. "I have no way to carry my sack. I have no pack animal, and the sack is too heavy for me to carry. I must not lose the grain. It is all I have."

C.H. lifted the sack and led Isis to a nearby place to sit and talk. She told him what had brought her to this unfortunate situation.

Ever since the family was reunited, they had lived in fear. "We had nightmares about being found and punished. We remembered what happened to our friend, the chief baker, and we knew the jealous king has an iron fist."

C.H. knew that they had no reason to be afraid because Tutmosis had become a changed man.

Tutmosis and Isis grew up together in the palace, and she was named after his mother. He was jealous because Hatshepsut was nice to Isis, but not to him. Her own daughters came first, Isis came second, and her husband's son and heir was treated like an outsider.

But that was another time, and now the people in Egypt talked about one God because Joseph had one God, and his God had great power. Pharaoh had learned about the power of Joseph's God.

But Phygsis and his family didn't know, so they were afraid. They were glad to be together, yet fear had kept them in hiding. And when the famine came upon the land, it became extremely hard for them to live.

"I saw the golden medallion," said C.H. "I figured Phygsis had come to buy grain. But that was a few days ago."

"I paid for the grain," Isis explained. "I wanted to accept it at a later time since I had no pack animal and I had no place to take it. But I accepted the grain today because I have nothing to eat. The medallion is worth more than one sack of grain, but I was afraid to bargain. So I have one sack, which is too heavy for me to carry, and I have no place to take it."

"Where are your parents?" asked C.H. "Where is Phygsis?"

"When we ran low on food, they refused to eat the little we had left," Isis said through her sobbing. "They gave me their food. Soon they both became sick and died. We sold all our belongings, even our house."

"You mean you have no place to live?" asked C.H.

"No place," replied Isis, sobbing.

C.H. sat in stunned silence for several minutes.

Finally, Isis stopped crying. "You once liked me."

C.H. did not respond.

"I heard the king gave you your choice of any woman from the palace who pleased you. Whom did you choose?"

"Huh?" said C.H., trying to refocus his thoughts. "Uh, no one. I didn't choose any woman from the palace."

"Would you have chosen me if I had not run away?" Isis asked.

Compassion filled C.H.'s heart. "That would be impossible. Sure, I like you a lot. You're a very lovely lady. But it would be impossible for me to choose you or anyone else. You may not understand this, but you see…I am a dead man."

She stared at him in total confusion.

"See, I'm here because I started this crazy search for a story that I could get published. But now I just want to live forever."

"Why do you say you are a dead man?" asked Isis.

"It's a long story," said C.H.

"Do you know my name?" asked Isis.

"Of course I do. It's Isis."

"Do you know where I got my name?" she asked.

"You were named after the king's mother, right?"

"Yes and no," said Isis. "The Egyptian goddess of fertility is named Isis, and we both received our names from her."

"Yeah, I knew that."

"The goddess Isis has a dead husband. His name is Osiris. She sprouts the grain and brings Osiris back to life each year." She gazed up at him. "Do you think I could bring you back to life?"

C.H. didn't know how to answer that question. The two of them sat silently for a long while. As his mind wandered, it came back to his gnawing question.

Thinking she might be able to help him find the answer, and wanting to change the subject to something less uncomfortable, C.H. said, "You grew up in the palace, right? You must have met a lot of important people in Egypt."

"Yes."

"I need your help in finding the third God."

She gave him a startled look.

"Let me put it this way. There is a Trinity in heaven, which means there's someone in Egypt who ranks in power with Pharaoh and Joseph. He has to be someone who loves both Pharaoh and Joseph, who is loved by Pharaoh and Joseph, and who is equal to them in power. Think of all the people you know in this country. Who would be equal in rank to Pharaoh and Joseph?"

"There is no one in Egypt like that. If there were, His Highness would hang him immediately. He is extremely jealous."

"Yeah, I've noticed."

"This thing that has happened in Egypt with Joseph is beyond this world," said Isis. "We have many gods, but Joseph's God has taken away all their power. Joseph's God is so powerful that Egyptians now have little faith in their own gods. Did you not see the harvests during the good years?"

"Are you kidding? I've seen grain beyond measure. All things are possible with God."

"Pharaoh has all the power in Egypt, and he has given equal power to Joseph. No one in Egypt can move a hand or a foot without Joseph's approval. Everyone in this country knows that."

C.H. grunted. "Well, there's someone out there, and I intend to find him."

The two sat silently for a moment. Then Isis returned the conversation to the things on her heart. "Why do you say you are dead? I can see you are alive."

"I don't think you can understand," said C.H. "It's really crazy. If you understood, you would know that I am dead. I am seeking the Bread of Heaven, and if I can find it, I will have a Savior, and I will live forever."

Isis thought for a moment. "Maybe I do understand. Everyone needs a savior. Including me. I have only one sack of grain, with no hope for more. The medallion is gone, and I have no more money. Unless I find a savior, I'm as good as dead…just like my parents." She began to weep.

"Even my beauty is gone. If someone were to choose me, he would be my savior."

Her words whacked C.H. like a clap of thunder. His mouth fell open, and he gazed at the beautiful lady sitting next to him as if he were seeing her for the first time. The longer he looked, the more compassion he felt for her.

Through a series of coughs and grunts, he forced out the words, "I choose you. I will be your savior."

Isis jumped to her feet, pulled C.H. to his feet, and smothered him with hugs and kisses. After a moment he took her shoulders and pushed her back to arm's length. "Hold on a minute. Let me think."

C.H. looked around and noticed some beggars among the people who were coming and going. Some of them had fainted. Those who were conscious begged money from those who were arriving to buy grain. They also begged grain from those who were loading their pack animals to leave.

"OK," C.H. said. "Give your sack to those beggars, and follow me."

CHAPTER 20

Benjamin Goes to Egypt

The famine in Canaan was so bad that grain from Egypt became a life-and-death matter. When the big family had eaten all their grain, Israel called his sons together and said, "Go again to Egypt and buy us a little more food."

Finally, Judah convinced his father. Judah stood in front of his father and shook his head. "No, not without Benjamin," he said. "The man emphatically warned us that we shall not see his face unless we bring our youngest brother back to Egypt. We cannot go back unless we take Benjamin."

"You should never have told the man that you had another brother," Israel said.

"There was something unusual about the man and his questions," Judah said. "He asked about you. He wanted to know if our father was still alive. He specifically asked if we had another brother. What were we to say?"

"Why were you so unthoughtful?" Israel wailed. "Why do you treat me so badly?"

"Look, send the boy with me and let us be on our way. I will make myself surety for Benjamin. Hold me accountable for him. If I do not bring him back to you and set him before you, let me bear the blame forever."

Israel looked up. He knew Judah was right.

"We have wasted too much time already," Judah said. "We could have been there and back twice by now. If we do not go soon, we and our children will die."

"Well," Israel said, "if it must be, then go."

So, ten brothers headed to Egypt, and this time the tenth was Benjamin. The brothers were like different men. They had hated their brother Joseph enough to kill him. What a change! Now they were taking Benjamin, their youngest brother, to Egypt like precious cargo that they would die to protect.

C.H. and Isis met at Joseph's house early in the morning. They had been instructed to help make ready for some kind of special affair. C.H.'s job was to make sure there would be plenty of beer and bread for a large crowd.

C.H. had trained Isis to sprout grain for making beer, and he gave her that responsibility in the Step Pyramid complex.

He said, "You sprout the grain. It is appropriate, since you were named after the goddess Isis who made the grain sprout to awaken her dead husband."

Isis smiled. "And so I will awaken you."

The young woman had regained the health and beauty she'd had when she used to dance for Pharaoh, before she and her family went into exile and she almost starved.

As he gazed at her, a question popped into C.H.'s mind. "What name did your mother give you when you were born?"

"She named me Ieb," said Isis.

"What does that mean?"

"It means heart," replied Isis. "When Egyptians die, their hearts can be weighed against the feather of Maat to see if that person is worthy to join Osiris in the afterlife."

"Really?" asked C.H. "So, since you are Ieb, and I am dead like Osiris, maybe you can join me in the afterlife."

"Don't tease about such important things," said Isis. "I want it to be true."

"You're right," said C.H. "It's not a joking matter. And I need to make a confession. This is really important." He took her hand. "Joseph's God is my God, too, and I want Him to be your God. You must believe in Him, and you must ask Him for the Bread of Heaven."

A fast chariot approached in a cloud of dust. It stopped in front of Joseph's house. The chariot driver, one of the sentries Joseph had posted to watch for the men from Canaan, jumped down and ran into the house.

C.H. and Isis followed to see what would happen.

"Was the boy with them?" Joseph asked the driver.

"Yes," replied the out-of-breath sentry. "They are on their way. They have been directed to come to your house, and they will be here soon."

CHAPTER 21

Joseph's Table

Joseph's house was abuzz with preparations for a special event. C.H. made himself appear busy while he kept a close eye on Joseph.

When the governor saw his brothers approach the house, he went outside and stood with his interpreter and his chief steward. His brothers came and stood before him.

"I'm not missing this," said C.H. as he followed along.

Joseph's heart was stirred as he looked at Benjamin for a long moment. Then he turned to his steward and said, "Bring the men into the house; they will be my guests and dine with me at noon. Make ready for a feast."

The men from Canaan were tent dwellers, and Joseph's house was very palatial. C.H. could see they were filled with suspicion and fear. Questions came to their minds. Were they being brought to Joseph's house for a reason?

I'll bet they are thinking about the money they stole.

They whispered to one another. Zebulon said, "What if they seize us and make us slaves? They may take our money and our donkeys."

Joseph left the men with his chief steward and went away, saying, "I will come back at noon."

The chief steward looked at the men, and said, "Welcome. Come inside."

The men stood still. Reuben said, "When we came the first time to buy grain, all our money was replaced in our sacks. We did not know this until we stopped at the inn. We opened a sack for some provender for our animals, and there was the money in the mouth of the sack. When we arrived home in Canaan we found all the money in full weight had been returned in the sacks."

The steward said, "Don't worry. Please, come inside."

"We don't know who could have done that," said Judah. "Now, have you brought us here because of this? If so, let us tell you now that we have come prepared to return the money. We also have come with additional money to buy more grain."

"No," said the steward. "You paid the money, and I received it. Please do not be afraid. It was your God, and the God of your father, who put the money in your sacks." He ordered a servant to care for their donkeys.

C.H. was close enough to hear the exchange, and he thought to himself, *Salvation is free. It's a gift from God.*

The steward said, "Here is someone you are anxious to see."

Simeon walked out of the house, and there was great rejoicing and lots of hugging as the brothers were rejoined with the freed prisoner. They felt more comfortable, and accepted the invitation to go into Joseph's house. They saw workers hustling about, making ready for a special feast.

Simeon helped his brothers take the gifts, which were brought for Joseph, into the house. There were bags of fruits, balm, honey, gum, resin, pistachio nuts, and almonds.

The red carpet of hospitality was out. Servants came with water for them to drink. They brought water and towels, and began to wash the brothers' feet.

As the aroma of food being cooked filled the house, Isis came quickly to C.H. and said, "Do you know what I just saw? The men from Canaan are getting their feet washed. A servant has brought water and has been told to wash the men's feet."

"That's a point of congruency," said C.H., who stopped what he was doing and stood up straight. Isis' words had triggered something in his memory. "The apostles got their feet washed too."

"What is a point of congruency?" asked Isis.

"Jesus washed His apostles' feet," said C.H.

A servant attending the entrance yelled out, "Zaphenath-Paaneah is coming." There was a hush and a moment of silence. Everything was ready. It was noon.

The brothers brought their gifts to Joseph, and they bowed with their knees to the ground before him.

Joseph said, "Please, stand up."

When the men were standing, Joseph said, "How are you all? Are you being treated well?"

They men were exuberant. "Yes," they replied in chorus.

Joseph asked, "Is your father well? You said that he is an old man. Is he alive and well?"

Levi said, "Your servant, our father, is well. He is alive and well, and thank you for asking." Again, they bowed.

Joseph looked at Benjamin. When he had last seen him Benjamin was a child. In the meantime Benjamin had become the father of ten sons. "Is this your youngest brother, the one you spoke of on your last trip to buy grain?"

Benjamin smiled an acknowledgment.

Joseph struggled to restrain his emotion. His mother, the beautiful Rachel, had died giving birth to the handsome young brother who stood before him. His words came hard. He grunted, "God be gracious to you my son."

Joseph turned quickly and hurried out of the room.

"What happened?" Isis whispered.

"I think he is crying," said C.H.

Joseph was overcome with emotion. He wept in private for a moment until he could regain his composure. Then he washed his face and returned to the large dining hall.

"Serve the meal," he instructed.

The dining room had three large tables. Joseph sat at a table by himself. The men from Canaan sat at a table by themselves, and a select group of Egyptians sat at the third table.

Racism prevailed in ancient Egypt. The Egyptians sat by themselves for a reason. While they loved and respected Joseph, they considered it an abomination to eat with Hebrews. Fourteen centuries before the crucifixion of Christ, the hidden secret of long ages past, which was revealed in Egypt, foresaw anti-Semitism in the world.

The brothers sat at the third table by themselves. With Simeon out of prison, and including Benjamin the brothers were now eleven in number. They sat at the table in order of their birth, with Reuben being the first and Benjamin being the last.

Six of them were Leah's children. They were Reuben, Simeon, Levi, Judah, Issachar and Zebulon. Leah also had a daughter, Dinah, but she was not there.

Dan and Naphtali were Bilhah's sons. Bilhah was Rachel's maidservant.

Gad and Asher were Zilpah's sons, and Zilpah was Leah's maidservant.

And then there was Benjamin.

The older brothers symbolized the morning. They preceded Joseph. Benjamin symbolized the evening. He came after Joseph.

Joseph came between the morning and the evening. He came at noon. The feast symbolized the Day of Pentecost. The food from Joseph's table symbolized the Bread of Heaven.

Those who preceded Jesus were the morning, and the Christians who came after him are the evening. Jesus came between the morning and the evening, and He poured out the Spirit on the Day of Pentecost.

The steward barked orders. Servants were assigned to bring prepared food from the kitchen to Joseph's table. "You serve to that table," he said to Isis as he pointed to the table where the Egyptians sat. "And you serve the Hebrews," he said to C.H.

Isis and C.H. took food from Joseph's table and began serving their tables. C.H. took portions first to Reuben, then to each man according to his age. Benjamin was the last to receive his portion.

When C.H. came to Joseph's table for the last serving that was for Benjamin, he said, "Shall I separate this?" The portion was enormous, five times the size of the other servings.

Joseph said, "Give the entire serving to the son of Israel."

Wow! thought C.H. *This is enough food for a horse. It's gotta symbolize something. I need to talk to Helper.*

CHAPTER 22

Relationships

When Jesus was eating the Last Supper He took the cup filled with wine and told His disciples to drink it. He said, "This cup is the new covenant in my blood, which is poured out for you." Luke 22:20 NIV

The Last Supper was foreshadowed by God's signs in ancient Egypt.

In his most profound prophesy, Jeremiah said, "'The time is coming,' declares the Lord, 'when I will make a new covenant with the house of Israel and with the house of Judah.'" Jeremiah 31:31 NIV

The great power from above who gave words to Jeremiah the prophet also gave ideas and motivation to Zaphenath-Paaneah.

C.H. knew what the Egyptians had been doing. It was a plan given by Joseph the previous evening.

When the meal was finally over, and the festive luncheon ended, Joseph arranged for the brothers to stay the night, and told them to be prepared to leave for home at the light of morning.

The plan was fixed, and it was from the same powerful hand that made the abundant crops grow in Egypt for seven years. The brothers would find surprises in their sacks, and the events of that day would foreshadow relationships in high places.

Joseph said, "Fill the men's sacks with grain. Give them as much as they can carry, and put their money back in the tops of their sacks in the same manner as before."

"Deja vu," said C.H. "Salvation is free."

"Take my silver chalice," Joseph said, "the one from which I drink wine, and put it in the sack of the youngest brother. Put it in the top of the sack with the money that was used to pay for the grain."

"But it is the one you use for divination," said the steward.

"Yes, it is a very special cup," Joseph confirmed.

The brothers had a great day. They were guests of honor, and they were invited to spend the night in Joseph's house. The following day began very early.

"This bread is delicious," said Reuben to Isis who was serving breakfast.

"Yes, it is delicious," said Levi. "I will have another serving. How did you make it?"

"My mother's recipe," said Isis. "It is made with pistachio nuts." Isis remembered the seven good years she spent with the mother she had believed to be dead.

Gad and Asher walked into the dining area where the men were eating. "We checked the animals," said Gad. "We are all set to leave. It will soon be light of day, and we must leave."

"Ready to go?" asked Simeon. "How could you be ready so quickly?"

"The Egyptians did it," said Asher. "When we came to the corral, they were there before us. The grain is loaded on our donkeys, and everything is ready."

"Yes, and they let all the animals drink their fill," said Gad.

"Did you check our water skins?" asked Reuben.

"Full," said Gad.

Jacob's sons prepared to head home. Benjamin had no way of knowing that he symbolized Christians of every race, color, nation, and tribe. Being Joseph's full brother, and the only son born after his father's name was changed to Israel, made him special. The forbearers of the houses of Israel and Judah were ready for the long trek back to Canaan.

But this trip would not take them to Canaan. Joseph said, "Make ready chariots, archers, spear bearers, and ax warriors. When the men have gone a distance well beyond the city, go after them and arrest them."

"You want us to go after the Hebrews and arrest them?" asked the steward.

"Yes," said Joseph. "When you overtake them, say, 'Why have you returned evil for good? Why have you stolen my lord's cup? Is it not from this cup that my lord drinks? Does he not indeed use it for divination? You have done wrong.'"

When the men from Canaan had traveled well beyond the city, the steward ordered, "Mount your chariots," and the fearsome Egyptian force drove at breakneck speed in pursuit.

C.H. hitched a precarious ride on a chariot. "This would make an old ambulance chaser feel right at home," he said.

When they overtook the brothers the steward repeated Joseph's words and accused the men of stealing.

Heartbreak descended upon the brothers like a clap of thunder. They were stunned and bewildered.

Judah said, "Why does my lord accuse us of such an evil thing? We, your servants, would never do such a thing. Do you not remember that we brought the money that we found in the tops of our sacks all the way from Canaan to return it to you? Why then would we steal silver or gold from your lord's house?"

The brothers stood helpless before the steward and his forces. Levi, a born fighter, said, "What can we do?"

Reuben said, "If your lord's silver and gold is found with any one of us, your servants, let the guilty one die. And when the guilty one dies, the rest of us will become my lord's slaves."

The steward answered, "No, the guilty one will become the lord's slave. The rest of you may go free."

The brothers all began to moan and speak of their innocence. They lowered their sacks to the ground for inspection.

From the eldest to the youngest, the brothers' sacks were searched, and in each sack was found the money that had been paid for the grain. Moans grew louder.

Finally, Benjamin's sack was opened. Everyone crowded about to watch. They elbowed their way to get a closer look.

The steward reached into the sack, grasped the silver cup and held it high in the air. The brothers recoiled as if the cup were a deadly viper. Some stumbled and fell to the ground.

Torturous screams rent the air. Anguish boiled up from their bellies, and they tore their clothes and pounded the earth. Ultimate evil had come upon them.

Joseph waited at his house. When he saw the prisoners being returned, he stood with his interpreter outside the house to meet them.

The brothers came, all falling to the ground, moaning and groaning as if they had great pain. They looked terrible in their torn and ragged clothes. Guilt and pain showed on their faces.

"What evil thing have you done?" asked Joseph. "Are you not aware that I have spiritual discernment, and that I can practice divination? You can steal gold and silver maybe, but did you think you could steal my personal chalice, the one from which I drink?"

Judah looked up from a nearly prostate position and said, "Oh, my lord, how can we speak to you? What can we say? What can we do?"

One after another the brothers begged forgiveness.

C.H. watched the confrontation from a position well removed. "They remember their sins against Joseph," he whispered to himself.

Judah asked, "Has God done this?"

"We are found out," cried Reuben. "God has found the guilt of your servants, and now we must all be your slaves."

Joseph said, "No, you will not all be my slaves. Only the one in whose sack was found my silver chalice will be my slave. He, and he alone, will be my slave. The rest of you shall return to your father."

The silver cup from which Jesus drank symbolized relationships. It symbolized a covenant with God and brotherhood with Jesus.

CHAPTER 23

The Savior Is Revealed

C.H. quickly sent Isis away. "We need sprouted grain to make more beer. Get some help with the heavy stuff, and I will come soon."

He wanted Isis out of harm's way, because the scene in front of Joseph's house was frightening. Eleven brothers were bowed to the ground in front of Joseph. The powerful vizier of Egypt had told them that Benjamin must be his slave.

"He will never get away with it," C.H. muttered to himself. He had come to understand Jacob's sons very well, and he knew that they would die before agreeing to give Benjamin over to slavery. "This may get bloody."

Judah stood up from his nearly prostate position. He said, "Oh, my lord, let your servant please speak a word. Give me your ears, and please do not be angry, for you have the glory of Pharaoh himself."

Joseph stood silent, and Judah continued. "You asked your servants, saying, 'Have you a father or a brother?' And we answered my lord, 'We have a father, an old man, and a young brother, the child of his old age. His brother is dead; he alone is left of his mother's children, and his father loves him.'"

From his somewhat obscured position, C.H. heard weeping. "It's a woman," he said, turning quickly to look all about. He saw no one and the sound went away.

Judah inched closer to Joseph. Almost word for word he repeated to Joseph all the conversations he and his brothers had shared with Egypt's governor. He repeated Joseph's own words back to him when Joseph demanded that Benjamin must be brought to Egypt or they would never see his face again.

While his brothers bowed their faces to the ground, Judah repeated all the conversations he and his brothers had with Jacob, their father, when they related the events of their trip to him. He told how their father's heart was broken. "His life is in danger because his life is tied to his beloved son."

No one moved or made a sound. Judah had the stage to himself. "Yes, we went back to our father, and we told him what you said."

C.H. muttered, "He thinks he's gaining Joseph's sympathy."

"And when our father said, 'Go again and buy us a little grain,' we said, 'We cannot go down to Egypt to buy grain unless our youngest brother goes with us. If we go without him, we will not see the man's face.'"

The guy would make a heck of a lawyer, thought C.H. *I think he's winning. Joseph looks moved.*

Judah continued, "Our father, your servant, said to us, 'My wife bore me two sons; one is left, the other has surely been torn to pieces by a vicious animal. There is not even a grave for me to visit. If you take this one from me, and harm comes to him, you will bring down my gray hairs in sorrow to Sheol.'"

Judah looked keenly at Joseph who had a tiny glisten in his eye. He took a deep breath and continued, "Therefore, upon our arrival, should we be allowed to return to our aged father at home in Canaan, and when your servant, our father, sees from afar that the boy is not with us he will surely die because his life is bound to the boy's life."

Judah fell to his knees respectfully and extended his right hand with the palm up. In his most persuasive voice, he said, "This, then, is what

I beg of you. Let the boy return to his father and make me your slave, because I became surety for the boy to my father."

He watched for Joseph's reaction to his proposal and continued. "I said to our father, 'If I do not bring him back to you, then I will bear the blame in the sight of my father all my life.' So I beg you, send the boy home with his brothers, and I will be your slave."

Joseph was beginning to lose control. Obviously, he was feeling all the pain and agony that was in Judah's heart, and great love and sympathy welled up in him. The brother who, so long ago, sold him into slavery was now offering himself to ransom his younger brother.

Suddenly, Joseph could not control himself. He shouted in a loud burst, "Send everyone away from me."

He waved to the Egyptians to leave. He looked at the steward of his house and shouted again, "Send everyone away from me." The Egyptians left the area, and Joseph and his brother remained in front of the big house.

His journalistic instincts flared, and C.H. moved quietly from his obscure position to another even closer to the men.

Joseph was too emotional to speak, and when everyone was gone except his brothers, he could not hold back. His chest heaved violently, and he wept so loudly that the Egyptians heard him from remote places in the house. Even the household of Pharaoh heard him, and they were filled with great wonder.

The brothers were caught off guard. C.H. could see that they were totally astounded. The powerful Egyptian who had imprisoned them and spoken so harshly was now standing before them weeping violently. Were Judah's words powerful enough to cause this? What amazing thing could have happened?

Levi, still prostrate, said, "Is he sick? Is he dying?"

Then Joseph calmed himself, and with some trouble he spoke to them in their own Hebrew tongue.

He said, "I am Joseph."

The brothers froze. No one breathed.

As quietness continued Joseph looked at his brothers for a long moment. All but Judah were still bowed to the ground, but their heads had jerked up and their wide eyes were searching Joseph. In unison their facial expressions asked, "What did he say?"

Joseph held his hands out toward them and repeated, "I am Joseph. Tell me again, is my father alive?"

The brothers stared at Joseph in disbelief. C.H. saw their mouths fall open, but nothing came out. What could this man be saying? Shock was written on their faces. *Why is this powerful Egyptian governor saying that he is Joseph?*

They all began to slowly and cautiously rise to their feet.

Finally, Joseph held out his hands and spoke again. "Come closer to me. I am your brother Joseph."

Judah rose to his feet, and the rest joined him as they began edging slowly toward the powerful Egyptian.

C.H. moved closer too.

Joseph said, "You sold me into Egypt; yes, I am that same brother. I am Joseph."

The brothers listened with wide eyes and mouths open, but they still could not speak.

"God sent me here for a reason," Joseph said. "He sent me here ahead of you to save your lives, so do not be angry at yourselves for what you did. God's plan has worked and I have become your savior."

The brothers gathered around Egypt's vizier. The words of the great Zaphenath-Paaneah began to sink into their ears. Eleven grown men began to cry.

"It clicked. They finally got it. The savior revealed himself to his brothers." C.H. watched the brothers as they accepted the fact that the governor was their lost brother Joseph. They jumped and slapped each other's backs amid hilarious shouting and laughing.

Joseph asked for quiet. "It was all God's plan. He sent me here before you," he said. He asked his brothers to sit down and listen because he had many things he wanted to tell them. "You are God's beloved remnant on earth, and you will have many survivors. God wants you kept alive, and He sent me here to preserve you. He made me as one with Pharaoh and lord of all his house. God made me ruler over all the land of Egypt. He filled our granaries with bountiful harvests, and now you and all your families may inherit the bread of Egypt."

"You must return to Canaan and bring all your families to Egypt," Joseph said. "Tell my father that the rope is coming after the bucket. Hurry now. Go up to my father and say to him, 'It is your son Joseph who speaks. We have seen him and we have heard his mouth speak. Come now to Egypt, and do not delay for your new home will be in Goshen.'"

"Bring your children, your grandchildren, your flocks, your herds, and everything you have, because you will live near me, and you will be safe from the severe poverty that reigns across the world."

Joseph said, "Tell my father how greatly I am honored in Egypt. Tell him there is abundant grain here, and I will provide. Tell him that the famine will be very sore in Canaan for five more years, and all who live there will be in great poverty, and there will be fainting and dying."

CHAPTER 24

The Nation of Israel

Did you hear?" asked C.H.

"Hear what?" replied the angel.

"They're coming," said C.H. excitedly.

"Who is coming?" asked the angel.

"Joseph told them to go home and bring the whole family to Egypt," answered C.H. "Hey, I knew that. The whole nation of Israel is coming to Egypt."

"Do you have a question?" asked the angel.

"Remember our first conversation?" asked C.H.

"Yes," replied the angel.

"You talked about a time when Israel was a child in Egypt."

"Yes, we discussed that," answered the angel.

C.H. was excited. He was a journalist at work. He had seen the wonders of God's signs in Egypt, and he had questions and things to talk about.

"I know what's gonna happen," said C.H.

"They are all coming to Egypt," agreed the angel who knew what C.H. was thinking.

"Sure, Jacob is going to bring the whole gang to Egypt, and the infant nation of Israel is going to live in Goshen," said C.H. "But that is not what I mean."

"What do you mean?" asked the angel.

"This is prophesy! I know what is going to happen many, many years from this moment of antiquity," explained C.H.

"Which is....?" asked the angel.

"They are coming to their Savior. Don't you see? Man, I can't wait. I can see the headlines now: 'The Nation of Israel Turns to Christ,'" yelled C.H.

"Yes, it will happen," said the angel.

"Do you think the Scripture agrees with me?" asked the excited journalist.

"Do you not remember what the prophet Hosea said about this?" asked the angel.

"No," replied C.H.

The angel said, "For the Israelites will live many days without king or prince, without sacrifice or sacred stones, without ephod or idol. Afterward the Israelites will return and seek the LORD their God and David their king. They will come trembling to the LORD and to his blessings in the last days." Hosea 3:4-5 NIV

C.H. clasped his hands behind his back and walked slowly in a big circle. It was his way to concentrate. "Yeah, I heard that David also symbolizes Jesus. So if that Scripture is true, it means...."

"That you are now on the right track," said the angel.

Joseph and his brothers spent hours talking. The brothers were still dazed. What a shock to learn that the great Zaphenath-Paaneah was their very own Joseph.

As they talked a servant came from Tutmosis and said, "If it pleases my lord, the king would like you to come speak with him."

The news had spread quickly to Pharaoh's house, and Tutmosis wanted all the details. When he learned of Joseph's father and the large family, which he knew something about already, he was instantly thrilled at the thought of being their host and bringing all of them to the safety of Egypt.

Joseph went to Pharaoh, and the king said, "Say to your brothers that they must load their animals and go back to Canaan. Tell them to take their father and all their possessions and come to me, so that I may give them the best of the land of Egypt, and they may enjoy the fat of the land.

"But there is more that you must tell them. They are to take wagons from the land of Egypt so that the wives and little ones may come down to Egypt in comfort. Tell them to give no thought to their possessions, for the best of all the land of Egypt will be theirs."

Joseph's heart was filled with great joy. He said, "It is Pharaoh who loves my family, and it is his grace that saves them."

So Joseph gave his brothers wagons and provisions for the journey. He called his wardrobe steward and ordered him to outfit each of his brothers with a splendid set of garments.

Again, the beloved child of the evening who symbolized brotherhood and sonship was treated very special. Joseph gave Benjamin three hundred pieces of silver and five sets of garments.

But Egypt's hospitality did not stop there. Joseph had his steward search out enough valuable things from Egypt to load ten donkeys, and these things were to be given to his father. Then he selected ten female donkeys and had them loaded with grain, bread, and provisions for his father for the journey back to Egypt.

Joseph said to his brothers, "Hurry to Canaan and to our father, and let there be no quarreling along the way."

Jacob, now called Israel, watched for his sons. He limped out to his favorite view area, as he did several times each day, and peered intently at the distant horizon. "They are past due. Surely something has happened," he said to Dinah.

Much of Dinah's time was spent keeping a protective eye on her aged father. She tried to comfort his aching heart, for Jacob had never stopped mourning the loss of his favorite son, Joseph. Each day he wept.

"They have had time to buy grain and return from Egypt two times. Something has befallen them."

"Your sons are strong men and able to handle trouble," said Dinah. "They will return, and Benjamin will be with them."

Her eyes were stronger than her father's, and so it was Dinah who first saw the returning brothers. "There," she said, pointing to something that had appeared in the distance. "Some dust and a caravan, but it is too large for our men. There are wagons. Our men took no wagons."

Jacob and Dinah stood anxiously waiting. As the caravan drew closer, the whole family heard the patriarch exclaim, "They are coming!"

Judah came ahead of the others, reassuring his father as he approached. "Your sons are all returned. Put your heart at ease. Benjamin is here, and we have brought gifts for our father."

But something was very different from what Jacob's eyes had expected. His sons were bringing home more than they had taken down to Egypt. He said, "They have wagons and twenty extra donkeys."

The rejoicing families rushed the men, and they all hugged and kissed one another. Eleven men strode around in their fine new garments like victorious heroes, and there was a celebration. Everyone, anxious to help, began to unload grain and tend animals.

Jacob remembered the last time his sons came back from Egypt. They came home with all their money that should have paid for the grain. This time they had come home with more surprises. He became very suspicious that something was not right. "What things did my sons do to gain all this excess?"

Finally, the brothers all went into Jacob's multi-pole tent and sat down to give him a report of their journey. They were bursting with eagerness to tell their father about the miracle.

Following family protocol, they waited for their father to speak first.

Jacob said, "Did your trip go well? How is it that you bring home more than your money could pay for?"

Gad could not wait. "Joseph is alive!" he exclaimed.

Reuben was the oldest, and he felt he should be the first to tell his mourning father about his favorite son, but he had no chance. In chorus the brothers jumped to their feet and began talking at the same time. "Joseph is alive! He is the governor!"

Jacob was stunned. He held his hands up with palms out, signaling for his sons to stop. "Why are my sons saying this? Have you lost your minds to say that Joseph is alive?"

"He is ruler over all the land of Egypt," said Reuben.

"He is the governor, and all the people bow down to him," said Judah.

Jacob paled and grew weak, and his spirit sank. Something crazy was causing his sons to say hurtful and deceiving things. He looked at Benjamin who bore no guile and no deceit, and even he was filled with joy and acknowledging that Joseph was alive.

Jacob felt faint. Two sons took him by the arms and led him out to look at his gifts. Asher ran ahead. He looked back at his father and said, "Joseph said to tell you, 'The rope is coming after the bucket.'"

Jacob loosed himself from his sons. He turned away and stopped listening. He stood looking into the distance for a few moments. He tried to comprehend all the things his sons were saying. As he turned back, all the brothers starting talking again, trying to convince their father.

A surge erupted in his spirit, and Jacob waved them away with both hands, saying loudly, "Enough! My son is alive. My son Joseph is alive."

His strength returned. He looked up to the sky, reached both arms high, and said, "Thank you. I must go see him before I die."

For two days all haste was made, and the whole family set out for Egypt. On the way they arrived at Beer-sheba, and Jacob had them stop there.

Jacob said, "Isaac is my father, and my father's God is the God in whom I trust, and I will offer sacrifices to Him."

During the night, after Jacob had made sacrifices, God spoke to him and said, "Jacob, Jacob."

Jacob answered and said, "Here I am."

God said to Jacob, "I am God, the God of your father; do not be afraid to go down to Egypt, for I will make a great nation of you in that place. I will go with you to Egypt, and I will also bring you up again; and Joseph's own hand shall close your eyes."

So the infant nation of Israel left Beer-sheba and traveled to Egypt. The sons of Israel with all their earthly possessions, and with Pharaoh's wagons to carry their large family made their way to their new home.

The thirty-three members of Jacob's and Leah's family who traveled to Egypt were:

Reuben and his four children,

Simeon and his six children,

Levi and his three children,

Judah and his three living children (two died in Canaan) and two grandchildren,

Issachar and his four children,

Zebulun and his three children,

and Dinah their daughter.

The sixteen children born to Jacob and Zilpah, Leah's handmaiden, were:

Gad and his seven children,

Asher and his four sons and one daughter and two grandchildren.

Jacob and Rachel had two sons, Joseph and Benjamin. Rachel's family included fourteen in all. Joseph was already in Egypt with two sons, Manasseh and Ephraim, who were born to him by Asenath, the daughter of Potiphera, the priest of On.

Benjamin had ten sons.

Jacob and Bilhah, Rachel's handmaiden, had a family of seven, which were:

Dan and his son Hushim,

Naphtali and his four sons.

So sixty-six direct descendants of Jacob, plus his sons' wives and servants, traveled to Goshen in the land of Egypt.

Joseph Purchased People for Pharaoh

C.H. stopped in his tracks. He gasped, grabbed Isis and pulled her back.

"Whoa! What the heck!" he exclaimed.

There in front of Joseph stood three huge men, so tall they dwarfed Joseph. The biggest one was about ten feet tall, and the other two were nearly as tall.

Isis clutched C.H. They started slowly backing away. "They are Zuzim," whispered Isis, "from Bashan. They are the tall ones."

A vague memory of something in the Bible about the giants of old flashed through C.H.'s mind.

Joseph's interpreter had a hard time talking with the big men. The big man who was talking kept repeating the same thing.

"What did he say?" demanded Joseph.

"He wants to exchange wine for grain," replied the interpreter. "But he has too little wine, and he wants too much grain."

At that moment one of the huge men collapsed. His companions tried catching him. They managed to break his fall and keep him from injury. The big man was faint from hunger. Famine was destroying the men and all their people. Many were dying. These three had come with wine to exchange for grain.

Joseph gave orders to show the men a place to rest, and he summoned C.H. to help. "Bring food and drink for these men."

More and more people were coming to buy grain, but they were bringing little or no money. There was no food in the whole region because the famine was severe. Egyptians and foreigners alike were wasting away because of the famine.

"Let us show hospitality to some of the dying people," said Joseph. "Feed them bread, give them drink and send them away. They may take no sacks with them without money to pay."

As brewmaster, C.H. was busy, and he felt great compassion for the famished people who were bringing their life savings to keep their families from starvation.

Grain held sway over life and death with both Egyptians and foreigners. Joseph collected all the money that was to be found throughout all the land, and he brought it to the king's treasury because all money accrued to Pharaoh.

People came in droves and bowed before Joseph, hungry and desperate but without money. One man stood and pleaded the people's case. "Give us food. Why should we die before your eyes? Our money is used up."

"You have livestock," said Joseph. "I will sell you food in exchange for your animals."

Day by day C.H. saw horses, cattle, sheep, goats, donkeys, and all manner of things being brought as payment for grain. But still many people died.

C.H. and Isis worked hard to help the people. They served bread and beer to those who came to buy, but they were forbidden from giving anyone sacks to take home. Both C.H. and Isis became depressed.

"The stench of death has come upon Egypt," said Isis.

"Yes," said C.H. "A cloud of sorrow and mourning has fallen upon us. I'm taking a break. I need to talk to the One who hears my prayers."

As C.H. left the Step Pyramid compound, heading for open country, a pungent odor stung his nostrils. "What is that smell?" he said. Just in front of him a wagon full of dead bodies had stopped to pick up another starved victim. C.H. turned to walk in a different direction.

When he was well away from the complex, his prayers became quite urgent. His compassion welled up and he beseeched God in a loud voice.

"Why?" he yelled. "Why will Joseph not just give food to the hungry? Look at them. They are all starving."

C.H. fell to his knees. "I need to talk to Helper."

When he rose to his feet, there stood his favorite angel.

"Helper," cried C.H. "You're going to give me a heart attack. God should put a bell on you.

"How may I help you?" the angel asked.

"Well..." stumbled C.H. "I want to talk about the Bread of Heaven... and other things." C.H. pointed to the complex. "There is plenty of grain, and Pharaoh is rich enough. Why are the people still starving?"

"You must read God's signs," said the angel.

"Signs? All I see is death."

"When you know the value of bread in Egypt, you will be more diligent to seek the Bread of Heaven," said the angel.

"Are you saying that this famine in Egypt symbolizes another famine?" asked C.H.

"Yes," said the angel. "Pharaoh had parallel dreams. He dreamt of cows and of corn, and his dreams foretold parallel famines."

"Pharaoh's dreams? Are you saying that seven good years followed by seven bad years in Egypt symbolize good times and bad times to come?" C.H. asked.

"Do you not remember the word of the Lord?" asked the angel. "It was the prophet Amos who said, 'The days are coming,' declares the Sovereign Lord, 'when I will send a famine through the land—not a famine of food or a thirst for water, but a famine of hearing the words of the Lord.'" Amos 8:11 NIV

Conditions throughout the land grew more difficult. One day many people came to the Step Pyramid. They assembled to stand before Joseph and plead for food. Others had died on the way, and some were fainting from hunger. Their grain was gone, their money and livestock were gone. They were all surely going to die.

As the people stood before Joseph, one man said, "We are starving with no way to pay. There is nothing left for our lord to receive in exchange for grain except our bodies and our land."

When C.H. saw the huge crowd gathering, he prayed, and Helper, his angel friend, came again. They listened as the starving people beseeched Joseph.

"Why should we die before your eyes? Purchase us," said the spokesman. "We, with our land, will be Pharaoh's slaves. Give us grain that we may eat and not starve."

Joseph agreed to give them grain in exchange for themselves.

"Good grief! They are selling themselves. This is too much," C.H. muttered. "Does God know about this? Does He know what the headlines will be: 'People Exchanged for Grain'?"

"God knows when a sparrow dies," said the angel. "You should pray to the Most High that you might hear a song from heaven."

"A song? You want me to hear a song?"

"Joseph purchased people for Pharaoh. What you see in Egypt points to a celebration in heaven when millions upon millions of angels sang about how Jesus purchased people for God. Pray that God will let you hear the song."

"What does the song say?"

"You are worthy to take the scroll and to open its seals, because you were slain, and with your blood you purchased men for God from every tribe and language and people and nation." Revelation 5:9 NIV

CHAPTER 26

C.H. Had a Dream

C.H. walked about the big Step Pyramid complex, deep in thought. He strolled through the colonnade with his hands clasped behind his back, as was his habit. "They are selling themselves," he said.

The crowd was large, and people stood in line to enter the sales booths. They were buying grain by selling themselves. Each person would sign an agreement, take his sack of grain, and leave. With each signature Pharaoh took possession of the man, his soul, and his land.

C.H. thought about his own condition. How astounding that his drowned body was lying on the banks of Lynx Lake, and God was granting him a chance to seek the Bread of Heaven.

"He must love me," C.H. muttered. "For sure, nothing is impossible for God."

The day had made him weary, and that evening as he slept, a vision came to him.

In his dream he heard the loud voice of a lion say, "Come," and there appeared a white horse. The white horse had a rider, and the rider held a bow. He was given a crown and told to roam the earth.

In his dream C.H. saw the rider on the white horse roam the earth for a thousand years. The rider went about filling spiritual granaries with truth, and as he rode, Christianity spread across the world. The granaries were filled to overflowing and beyond measure. C.H. observed the same powerful hand from above that made the crops grow in Egypt for seven bountiful years.

Christianity rose to the very top of powerful governments. Laws, constitutions, declarations, and covenants were written by men using God's laws as their model and their guide. God was enshrined in currencies, monuments, halls of government, and memorials.

Institutions were started to advance the cause of Christianity. Churches sprang up like weeds. Nations like Italy, Spain, France, Germany, England, and the United States had strong Christian principles guiding their national standards of ethics and morality. Christianity was strong in Russia for a thousand years.

C.H. watched faith sink deeply into good soil. Fires were ignited in the hearts of men. Christ was King.

Eventually, an east wind began to blow. In his dream C.H. joined a cloud of witnesses and watched a mighty angel descend into a bottomless pit. The angel entered the abyss and stood in front of the doors of the dungeon. He prepared to open the doors and release the prisoner. Cherubim sentries relaxed their flashing swords and departed the abyss.

Aghast and frightened, the witnesses heard the creaking of the rusty doors being forced open. Wind gusted and swirled, blowing dust and debris, and there came a stench and a loud hissing sound.

A silhouetted figure appeared dimly in the dust, and a bird of prey emerged slowly from the east. As the chains came off, he snorted his rage, flexed his muscles, and spread his wings. Fully awake, he surged forth, ready to soar. He would roam the earth, seeking whom he might devour.

A war ensued. The bird took command of his hoard. They had been without his leadership for a thousand years. He taught them to use cunning and guile to fight against the man called by God from a far country. Blood dripped from his carnivorous beak as he sucked the blood of saints.

The great dragon caused extremely ugly cows to come up out of the Nile. He soared above society's most vulnerable, and like a huge net, he cast a spirit of rebellion over large numbers of young people. He caused them to don the appearance of evil and derange their hair, their faces, and their clothing. They insulted their bodies with crude piercings and graffiti. They sang rebellious songs and rejected traditional values. Love grew cold.

Great crowds fell under the evil bird's spell and chose altered cultures and lifestyles empty of faith, wisdom, and truth. Men turned away from truth and filled their minds with fantasies that tickled their ears.

Wormwood fell from the sky and beguiled men with false doctrine to build the temple of God. Corrupted theology, like vermin infesting the granaries, caused men to exchange good for evil. They called upon Allah and prayed to the Most High. But they did not know Joseph, so they received no bread.

An extremely sore famine came upon the world, and only those who had access to the granaries of truth were able to feed on the Bread of Heaven. No one could buy bread without permission from the man called by God from a far country. His name means "the one who furnishes the nourishment of life."

The white horse galloped through the fray and across the ramparts for a thousand years. The rider's robe was stained with blood, and he was scarred from battle. The fight made him steadfast and strong. He was awesome and fierce in battle, and he garnered many crowns.

The man from a far country gave the rider a new name that only he knew, and he branded his horse. On the hindquarters of the white horse was branded: Lord of Lords and King of Kings.

Many white horses were spawned, and they followed closely, with a vast multitude of those who received bread from the granaries of truth.

CHAPTER 27

The Spirit Not Yet Given

As he dreamed, C.H. began to call out loudly, "Dear God, I'm searching for the Bread of Heaven. May I have some?" When there was no answer, he yelled, "May I just see the Bread?"

Suddenly, there appeared a large dining room that looked familiar. C.H. recognized it as being in Joseph's house, and he remembered how the brothers had come and sat at the table in order of their birth.

A man entered and sat at the table. It was Reuben, the eldest of Jacob's sons, and he looked like one of the many starving Egyptians who were barely hanging to life. Each brother came, one at a time, and sat at the table. When one was seated, another would come and take his seat, each representing a later time period. All came in and took a seat except Benjamin.

A select group of Egyptians entered and sat at another table, and they too looked to be near death from starvation.

C.H. said, "Why are these men so hungry? Give them some bread."

He heard the pounding of hoof beats, and a rider on a white horse approached. The rider was the apostle Paul. He rode among the tables and looked at all those who were waiting for bread. He said, "Death reigned from the time of Adam to the time of Moses, even over those who did not sin by breaking a command." Romans 5:14 NIV

Paul spurred his horse and rode away.

An angel appeared and announced, "There is faith on earth." A door opened, and a group of people came into the room and sat at the table. C.H. recognized Abel and Enoch. In came Noah, followed by Abraham and Isaac. Moses came in. The prostitute Rahab came in, Gideon, Baraki and Samson joined them, followed by Jephthah, David, and Samuel.

C.H. cried out, "They are faithful. Give them bread!"

Another white horse galloped up, and the rider moved among the tables. The rider waved his arm over all the people and said, "These were all commended for their faith, yet none of them received what had been promised." Hebrews 11:39 NIV

C.H. heard a voice in Ramah. It was weeping and greatly mourning. He had heard the same woman softly weeping before. It was Rachel, and she refused to be comforted because her children were no more.

C.H. began to weep. He felt great compassion for Rachel. "Oh, Joseph," he wept. "Oh, Benjamin, you are no more."

The prophet Jeremiah appeared and approached C.H., and with his hand he signaled C.H. to stop weeping. He said, "A voice is heard in Ramah, mourning and great weeping, Rachel weeping for her children and refusing to be comforted, because her children are no more. This is what the Lord says: 'Restrain your voice from weeping and your eyes from tears, for your work will be rewarded,' declares the Lord. 'They will return from the land of the enemy. So there is hope for your future,' declares the Lord. 'Your children will return to their own land.'" Jeremiah 31:15-17 NIV

His sadness vanished and C.H. was thrilled. He said, "I get it! God will call His Son out of Egypt." At that moment he heard chimes, and he knew it was noon.

Joseph came in, followed by Benjamin. Joseph appeared as a slain lamb, and he said, "If anyone is thirsty, let him come to me and drink.

Whoever believes in me, as the Scripture has said, streams of living water will flow from within him." John 7:37-38 NIV

C.H. said, "Hold it a minute. What do you mean?" He looked at a teacher and asked, "What did he mean by that?"

The teacher stood among them and said, "By this he meant the Spirit, whom those who believed in him were later to receive. Up to that time the Spirit had not been given, since Jesus had not yet been glorified." John 7:39 NIV

"Jesus?" C.H. asked.

As C.H. looked at Joseph, he saw him begin to change.

"What the heck? He's morphing," cried C.H.

The figure was dressed in a white robe reaching down to his feet, and there was a golden sash around his chest. His head and hair were white like wool, as white as snow. His eyes were like blazing fire.

"That's not Joseph. It's Jesus!" said C.H.

The figure's feet were like bronze glowing in a furnace, and his voice was like the sound of rushing waters. In his right hand he held seven stars, and out of his mouth came a sharp double-edged sword. His face was like the sun shining in all its brilliance.

Benjamin stood behind Abraham and placed his hand on Abraham's shoulder. "He redeemed us in order that the blessing given to Abraham might come to the Gentiles through Christ Jesus, so that by faith we might receive the promise of the Spirit." Galatians 3:14 NIV

Benjamin began morphing. C.H. yelled out, "Hold it. What's happening?" Suddenly, he was looking at Benjamin's great-great-grandson, the apostle Paul, standing among a crowd of Gentiles.

Servants began taking food from Jesus' table and serving it to those who sat at the tables. C.H. watched the servants bringing food. They were going right to the throne of God, and they were dipping golden censors into the fire before the throne and bringing it to Jesus.

"It's not bread made of grain," cried C.H. "It's fire. The Bread of Heaven is fire! The Bread of Heaven is the Holy Spirit of God!"

Each person sitting at a table was given a smoldering cinder to replace his heart. Worth more than all the world's riches, it was a free gift from God, and it was a living entity that would never die.

Like an issue from a sire, who would give the gift of life to his child, the burning ember imparted a quantity of God to the one to whom it was given. Yet it was only a deposit, or an embryo, of the fire that was promised.

A group of riders on white horses began moving among the tables, and they were preaching, "Fan it, fan it, fan the fire. Start the sanctifying process. Fan it, and belong to God, your Father, who has conceived you."

C.H. saw a man who fanned his burning ember until it burst into flames. The more he fanned the ember, the more it grew, and the more it grew, the more he changed into a new person. A flame stood over the man's head, and he received revelation from God. C.H. saw how God's communication system works. Joy, peace, wisdom, and understanding were downloaded into the man.

C.H. watched the man's transmutation. His physical body, decimated from age, became nothing but a tent, but the inner man bloomed like a flower into a vibrant new species. He became a radiant spiritual person who would never die, and whose godly genes were daily conforming him into the familial appearance of Jesus.

For a while, the man kept his same physical appearance. But then a rider on a pale horse came and circumcised the old physical body, and a beautiful new creature that was neither male nor female appeared. He was declared to be God's son, given a new name, and released to soar the fragrant heights of heaven.

"Oh, dear God," said C.H. as he awoke from his dream. He left his bedroom quickly because he felt the urgent need to pray, and he did not want to awaken Isis.

Outside he continued, "Help me. Please help me. I need the Bread of Heaven. I need fire. I need Your Spirit."

When he looked up from his prayer, the angel, Helper, was standing before him.

"Your time in Egypt is finished," said the angel.

"What?" cried C.H.

"Do you wish to continue your search for the Bread of Heaven?"

"Yes, of course, but–"

"You have seen many things in Egypt," said the angel. "The Lord God has shown you all you came here to see, and your faith should be strengthened. Now it is time to leave."

"I can't leave yet. There is someone in Egypt that I have not found. I am looking for a very special person. I must find him before I leave here."

"Who is that person, and why must you find him?" asked the angel.

"Somewhere in Egypt is the person who symbolizes the third God–you know, the Spirit. The Holy Ghost."

The angel shook his head. "To even search beyond His testimony is a wavering of faith."

C.H. looked in the direction of the bedroom where Isis lay sleeping. "I can't go," he said.

"Why not?" asked the angel.

"I have responsibilities here," he replied, thinking of his beautiful tattooed lady.

"You are a dead man," said the angel. "You have no future in Egypt. Follow me."

CHAPTER 28

Confess Him, Confess Him

A conflicted C.H. followed the angel. "Where are we?" he asked. "This place is called Golgotha," replied the angel.

They walked up an incline and eventually came to a place where three crosses were silhouetted against the horizon. Three men were being crucified, and there was a crowd around them.

As they approached the crowd, C.H. could hear mindless mocking and taunting. Some men struck the one on the middle cross and spat on him. The stench of mortality was in C.H.'s nostrils. Heavy darkness overhung the area and cast a sinister aura.

C.H. heard an echo from ancient Egypt that sounded like the Midianites asking Joseph, "How did you get into this pit with no way out?"

He looked at the men on the other two crosses. One looked like wine that lives, and the other looked like bread that dies. The one in the middle looked like Joseph, who was hated by his brethren.

The sky grew darker and darker until it was as black as midnight, yet it was the middle of the day.

As C.H. came close enough to see the faces of the men on the crosses, he heard another echo. It was Jesus speaking to Peter, asking, "Who do you say that I am?"

He heard Peter respond, "You are the Christ, the Son of the living God." Matthew 16:16 NIV

C.H. became sick, and he could no longer look at the men on the crosses.

"Why are we here?" he asked the angel.

"You prayed for a story about Jesus."

A Roman soldier took a spear and pierced Jesus' side. Water and blood gushed out from Him and flowed, mingled down. The red of blood mixed with the blue of water to make purple, and a royal issue flowed from Jesus. Dead men arose from their graves and walked about.

God had told the people to make a curtain to go in the temple to shield the Most Holy Place. He said, "Make a curtain of blue, purple and scarlet yarn and finely twisted linen, with cherubim worked into it by a skilled craftsman." Exodus 26:31 NIV

The curtain was a heavy woven material with embroidery. It was about four inches thick, and no man could tear it. It was blue on one end and red on the other. Where blue and red came together in the middle, it was purple.

At the instant when Jesus gave up His spirit and died, the heavy curtain was torn from top to bottom, right through the middle and right through the purple. A royal issue of the blood from Jesus opened a royal entrance into the holy place where God lives.

C.H. looked back at the cross and tried to repeat the words of Peter: "Thou art the Christ, the Son of the living God." But the words would not come out.

"I must confess him," said C.H.

"You are dead. It is too late," said the angel.

Darkness descended upon his spirit. He felt himself falling into the black pit of death. Down, down he fell. Finally he stopped at the place where he first saw the shimmering light of the angel.

Extreme pain seized C.H. and he could feel men pushing on his chest. Someone was trying to blow air into his lungs. He looked down and saw the crowd surrounding his body. They were talking. He heard one say, "I think he is gone." Another said, "He's gone, all right."

A force was drawing C.H. to his dead body, and he could not resist. He knew that once he reentered his body, he would be dead forever.

At that moment he heard the angel say, "Stop! Do not reenter your body. The Lord God has not forsaken you."

CHAPTER 29

God Called a Man from a Far Country

"Follow me," said the angel.

C.H. followed the angel, and they came to some men who were standing in a group listening to another man who was addressing them.

"They can neither see you nor hear you," said the angel.

"I don't get it," said C.H. "Why are we back in Egypt, and why is Joseph talking to his brothers again?"

"We're not in Egypt," said the angel. "We are in Canaan. That is Jesus. He has risen from the grave, and He is talking to His disciples."

C.H. sucked in a quick, startled breath. "Oh, my gosh! That is Jesus. He's alive."

"He has breathed the Spirit upon His disciples to open their minds. He wants them to understand what is about to happen. Listen, and you will hear a great promise. He is going to send the Bread of Heaven."

The angel had brought C.H. to a time and place where he could watch the ascension of the risen Savior and hear His farewell to His disciples.

"He has led them here to the Mount of Olives. This place is near Bethany, a Sabbath day's walk from Jerusalem. Watch carefully, and you will see an astounding thing happen."

Jesus said, "I am going to send you what my Father has promised; but stay in the city until you have been clothed with power from on high." Luke 24:49 NIV

All eyes were fixed on Jesus. C.H. knew something was about to happen. But what could it be?

Suddenly, right before their eyes, Jesus rose up from the ground into the air. With open arms He looked back at His disciples and blessed them. Then all eyes watched as He was transported by a cloud from earth to heaven.

"God has called a man from a far country," said the angel.

C.H. finished the angel's thought. "To fight against a famine."

"Right," confirmed the angel.

C.H. was becoming familiar with the words of Isaiah: "From the east I summon a bird of prey; from a far-off land, a man to fulfill my purpose. What I have said, that will I bring about; what I have planned, that will I do." Isaiah 46:11 NIV

CHAPTER 30

Heaven's Open Door

The angel said, "Follow me."

C.H. followed him to a high place with a panoramic view looking through an open door. It was the same door through which the apostle John overlooked a giant heavenly scene.

"Look," he whispered, "there is the apostle John." It was the Lord's day and John was in the Spirit.

C.H. was about to speak to John when the angel said, "He can neither hear you nor see you."

C.H. could tell that John was terrified. He wanted to help. He followed John's gaze and caught sight of a huge throne with One sitting on it. Bursts of power and glory emanated from Him. The One on the throne appeared as jasper and carnelian, but no one could look at His face. His face was a thousand times brighter than the sun.

The angel cautioned, "Don't look at the One on the throne. You may die."

The host of heaven was assembled before the throne. There were millions upon millions of angels and heavenly creatures, and the scene was like a giant setting for a celebration. C.H. could feel the worship and excited anticipation that rose from the vast sea of creatures.

He shuddered. He felt chill bumps, and he remembered the moment in Egypt when Pharaoh was about to declare Joseph to be the new governor. His eyes searched the giant scene, trying to observe everything. He said, "I know what's up. There will be a coronation."

Suddenly, behind John, a voice spoke like a trumpet. It told him to write on a scroll what he saw and heard. The voice said, "Write, therefore, what you have seen, what is *now* and what will *take place later.*" Revelation 1:19 NIV (emphasis added)

In His right hand, the One on the throne held a scroll that was written on both sides. The scroll was sealed with seven seals. A modern-day equivalent would be seven sealed envelopes, each containing part of a will.

The scrolls contained all the matters about which John was to write. They contained what is *now* and what would *take place later.* C.H. made the connection, and he felt his body quiver. In ancient Egypt, the "now" secrets and the "take place later" secrets were sealed in Pharaoh's mind.

"Very profound," said C.H. as he looked at the scroll in God's right hand and thought about the mysterious dream once locked in Pharaoh's mind when the whole land of Egypt faced starvation. Now the whole world faced another kind of famine.

The first side of the scroll related to existing conditions and world order. God's eternal plan had been in effect since before the creation of the world.

When Joseph became governor, the fields, the workers, the seed, and the great inundation already existed. The first side of the scroll could be called the "*now*" side.

The second side could be called the "*take place later*" side. That plan called for a new ruler to come and open the scrolls, and to have authority over both heaven and earth. Trumpets would sound, and the new King would wage war against the bird of prey from the east.

There would be a morning and an evening; the King's domain would have seven good years and seven bad years. The King would come at noon and there would be bread for all his brothers. C.H. felt sure that he had seen the shadow that foretold all these matters.

From the throne came blinding flashes of lightning, deep bone-shaking rumbles and mighty claps of thunder. Certainly, there could be none like the One who sat on the throne. C.H. was gripped with hypnotic awe. He was in the presence of the almighty God, the One and Only, who made the earth tremble, and nations could not endure His wrath. *How great are His signs,* C.H. thought, *and how mighty are His wonders!*

"Do you know the first commandment?" asked the angel.

"I—I think so," stuttered C.H.

The angel pointed to the One sitting on the throne. "Love the Lord your God with all your heart and with all your soul and with all your mind. This is the first and greatest commandment." Matthew 22:37-38 NIV

Living creatures surrounded the throne, and they never stopped worshiping Him.

Before the throne were seven blazing torches, which symbolized the sevenfold Spirit of God.

"Where is the third God?" asked C.H. "Didn't you say I could see Him?"

"Do you not know the Scripture?" asked the angel. "If you are looking for the Spirit of God, look there, in front of the throne. Do you see those mighty blazing torches? Those seven torches are also called the altar of God. You can feel warmth and peace radiating from them."

C.H. felt drawn to the blazing torches. He sensed that extreme joy was divinely connected to the torches and just beyond his reach.

"This is what Jesus meant," he said. "It's the promise. This is what His Father promised Abraham. Man, I can't wait."

Thoughts of his dream returned to him, and he remembered John saying that the Spirit had not yet been given because Jesus had not been glorified.

"I saw that in my dream," he said to the angel. "The sevenfold Spirit of God. Servants were dipping golden censers into the altar and filling them with fire. It was the Bread."

C.H. thought about the huge granary where he'd worked. "Grain, grain beyond measure." He looked at the torches and said, "Spirit without limit and beyond measure."

He became totally fascinated by the torches. He pointed to them, and asked, "Living water?"

The angel nodded. "The Spirit has not been given because Jesus has not yet been glorified."

C.H. kept a vigilant eye on John. "Poor guy," he said. "What is going on in his mind?"

John was frightened and concerned. He was focused on the scroll. What could it mean?

Suddenly, C.H. sensed a great problem in heaven. He vividly recalled the problem that had come upon Egypt many years before, when a secret was locked in Pharaoh's mind and the enemy was an east wind that would devastate the bread of life in all the land.

For a moment C.H. relived the time he stood in front of Pharaoh, hoping the king would be excited about a golden medallion. But the furrowed brow of Pharaoh had indicated he had a more serious problem.

Now, the problem in heaven was centered around the scroll and the need for someone to open it and to reveal God's will. Who could open the scroll?

As C.H. focused closely on the scroll, he began to hear echoes from long ages past. He heard promises given to Abraham that would be kept through the work of the Spirit. He heard Joseph interpret Pharaoh's dreams and speak of good times and bad times.

The journalist's instincts kicked in. "I think the ghosts of extremely ugly cows will come up out of the Nile," he muttered. "I see it now. God wrote history in reverse. I saw the shadow before the light appeared."

There was suspense in heaven. What was in the scroll? Who could open it? These became pressing questions. Like a giant wave, great

anxiety swept the heavenly scene. The open question lay before all creation, "Who can open the scroll?"

John began to weep.

War, C.H. said to himself. *There will be war! It will be a life-and-death battle between a bird of prey from the east and a man from a far country who will do God's purposes.*

C.H. looked at John. His weeping increased, and tears came to C.H.'s eyes.

Just as Pharaoh had a problem finding someone who could interpret his dreams, now in heaven no one could take the scroll and open its seals. Pharaoh had searched high and low, including all the magicians and wise men of Egypt, before he found a man from a far country who could open the mystery locked in his mind.

John is really upset, thought C.H. He yelled out, "Somebody open it. We need to find out what is now, and what will take place later."

He looked at the angel and asked, "Will there be a search, like Pharaoh demanded?"

"Yes," replied the angel.

C.H. spread his arms wide as he looked at the vast heavenly host. "How many of these know what is written in the scrolls?"

"The scrolls contain the deep things of God," said the angel. "Do you not know the Scripture? 'The Spirit searches all things, even the deep things of God.'" 1 Corinthians 2:10 NIV

A God-driven search went forth. Searchers went everywhere. They searched the earth, they searched the sea, they searched under the sea. They searched all of heaven, and the word went forth, "Let there be no place that is not searched."

When every corner of every space was searched, there was no one found who could even look inside the scroll.

"What a shocker!" said C.H. "The third God should at least be spiritual enough to look inside the scroll."

"It is a sign," said the angel.

C.H. clutched himself in pain. He looked at the angel and said, "Are you trying to tell me that there is no holy Trinity? Do you have any idea how much trouble I would cause if I were to write a story saying there is no holy Trinity?"

"Did you come here to argue over words? Or do you wish to read God's signs?"

Things grew desperate in heaven. C.H. watched John's chest heave with heavy sobs.

Suddenly, a loud voice startled John. A mighty angel spoke to all creation. "Who is worthy to break the seals and open the scroll?" The echo went about heaven and throughout the earth. "Who? Who?"

"Hey," C.H. said "God knows who can open the scroll. Why was this search necessary?"

"Jealousy," replied the angel. "Do you not remember that He is a jealous God? Jealous is His name. By this search He has expunged all claims, He has swept the deck, He has emptied all offices, He has nullified all crowns and thrones and positions of authority, and He has burned all banners."

The Greatest Day

The Spirit of God has visited men throughout history, and we have stories of the many ways He interacted with His people. They were inspired to write, to speak, to see visions and have dreams. The Hebrew noun for Spirit is *ruah,* which occurs 377 times in the Old Testament. But in all of those occurrences, *ruah* was never given to men as bread from heaven.

In all the times that fire symbolized God's Spirit, and all the fires of sacrifices and burnt offerings, and all the times that the Scriptures mentioned God and His Spirit, *ruah* never produced children.

When men of God had things revealed to them by the Spirit, and when they spoke by the Spirit, no one, including all the great men of faith, had ever received the gift of the Holy Spirit internally, in a personal way to produce a newborn child.

Ruah did not sire children for God.

If Moses, being justified by faith, had stood on a very high place when the Spirit of God appeared to be burning the whole mountain, and if he had looked out over all the tribes of Israel, even if he had looked out over all the people in the world, he would not have seen a single person, including himself, who had been sanctified by the Spirit, because the sanctifying Spirit had not yet been given.

An elder came and spoke to John. The weeping apostle was very upset. He, more than anyone, knew that the life-giving Spirit had not been poured out, and C.H. knew exactly what bothered him. Someone had to take the scroll from the hand of God and open the seals.

This was the day of promise, a day of great expectation. The historical moment had arrived but John's happy anticipation had turned to wrenching fears.

The elder said to John, "Do not weep. See, the Lion of the tribe of Judah, the Root of David, has triumphed. He is able to open the scroll and its seven seals." Revelation 5:5 NIV

Suddenly, the Lion of the tribe of Judah stood in the center of the throne, encircled by the four living creatures and the elders. He appeared as a slain lamb, and all the eyes of heaven focused on Him.

The Lamb had seven horns and seven eyes, which symbolized the seven spirits of God sent out into all the earth.

C.H.'s body jerked when he saw the Lamb.

"Whom do you see?" asked the angel.

"Wow! It's Jesus," he exclaimed.

C.H. did a quick double-take. He looked at the torches in front of the throne, and he looked back at the Lamb. "His eyes are replicas of the torches."

"He symbolically sees through His Father's eyes," said the angel. "He can search the deep things of God."

C.H. was enthralled by the torches and by the Lamb. An outburst of strange language erupted from him. He was surprised at what he had just done. "What was that? I said something, but what?"

"You spoke in a heavenly language," replied the angel.

"I know what I was thinking, but I have no idea what I said," said C.H.

"Do you wish an interpretation?" asked the angel.

"Yes," replied C.H.

"You quoted Scripture," said the angel. "You repeated God's testimony when He identified Himself, and when He identified His Son."

C.H. looked at the One sitting on the throne, being careful not to look at His face. His being was breathtaking beyond measure. C.H. felt as if he were being melted in a furnace.

Deep and powerful rumblings emanated from the throne, and the rumbling shook the entire heavenly scene. Lights brighter than the sun flashed in all directions. C.H. trembled, grasped in total awe.

"Would you please tell this poor dead man what he uttered, and what the Most High testified," C.H. requested.

"The One who sits on the throne said, 'I am God, and there is no other; I am God, and there is none like me.'" Isaiah 46:9 NIV

"I said that?" asked C.H. He pointed at the Lamb. "What did I say about Him?"

The angel said, "When Jesus was baptized, heaven was torn open, and God spoke from a cloud and said, 'This is my Son, whom I love; with him I am well pleased.'" Matthew 3:17 NIV

C.H.'s eyes panned the great heavenly scene. He saw four living creatures around the throne, and they were praising God. One had the face of a lion, one had the face of an ox, one had the face of a man, and the last one had the face of an eagle. "Wow! Who are they?" asked C.H.

"They are God's creatures," said the angel. "They are servants, and they are powerful to do the Lord's bidding. They will call upon mighty forces to roam the earth."

"Whom else do you see?" continued the angel.

C.H. counted. "I see twenty-four men sitting on twenty-four thrones with golden crowns."

"They are elders," said the angel. "Watch. They are removing their crowns."

"Why?" asked C.H.

"They are surrendering all glory, power, and authority. They are prepared to surrender their lives and to give themselves as slaves to the new King."

"Whom else do you see?" asked the angel.

"I see the souls of some dead people under the altar. Do you see them?" asked C.H.

"Yes, I do," said the angel. "They are morning people who have been sealed."

"Do you think Jacob and his family are there?"

"God seals whom He pleases," replied the angel.

Then, in an instant, all the eyes in heaven focused on Jesus as He took the scroll from the right hand of God. Astounding! It was the greatest empowerment of glory and authority that had ever happened. Joseph's promotion in Egypt was no comparison.

When Jesus took the scroll from the right hand of God, a celebration erupted in heaven. It was an outburst to end the centuries of waiting of all creation.

The host of heaven and the elders, without their crowns, fell down before Jesus to acknowledge His kingship.

C.H. fell to his knees. There was not a hint of conflicting authority.

At the moment when Jesus took the scroll, the four living creatures joined the twenty-four elders and fell down before the Lamb. Each one had a harp, and they were all holding golden bowls full of incense, which symbolized the prayers of the saints.

All of heaven joined their voices in singing. There were happy songs of praise and rejoicing, and Jesus was glorified by a brand new song. Resonant baritone voices, strong tenor voices, and voices of every description blended together and sang:

"You are worthy to take the scroll and to open its seals, because you were slain, and with your blood you purchased men for God from every tribe and language and people and nation. You have made them to be a kingdom and priests to serve our God, and they will reign on the earth." Revelation 5:9-10 NIV

C.H. joined in the song. He recalled how Joseph had purchased all the people in Egypt for Pharaoh.

With eyes and ears on high alert, C.H. watched the coronation and listened to the voices of many angels, numbering thousands upon thousands, and ten thousand times ten thousand. It was awesome. The angels encircled the throne, the living creatures, and the elders. They raised their voices so that they could be heard on earth, on the sea, and everywhere there was an ear to hear. They sang:

"Worthy is the Lamb, who was slain, to receive power and wealth and wisdom and strength and honor and glory and praise!" Revelation 5:12 NIV

C.H. was full of joy. He sang loudly, and he remembered Joseph suddenly receiving power in Egypt, and every knee was required to bow to him. "Let no one move a hand or a foot without His approval," he cried out.

The singing became louder and more joyous. God was included in the songs and the praise. Every creature in heaven and on earth and under the earth and on the sea and all that was in them sang:

"To him who sits on the throne and to the Lamb be praise and honor and glory and power, for ever and ever!" Revelation 5:13 NIV

Every mouth in heaven shouted, "Amen." The sound rattled creation and shook the earth, and everyone fell down and worshiped.

C.H.'s spirit was rapturous.

John prepared to write.

Jesus held the scroll and stood ready to open it. There was no more waiting. When the Lion of the tribe of Judah opened the first seal, one of the four living creatures, the one with the face of a lion, said, "Come!"

C.H. was startled at the sound of the living creature's loud, thundering voice. It trumpeted like furious waves of water crashing upon the rocks.

A white horse stood before John. Its rider held a bow, and he was given a crown. The white horse galloped off. Its rider, with his new crown, went on a worldwide mission to sow and reap for his King. He rode as a conqueror bent on conquest.

"Oh, yeah!" exclaimed the excited journalist. "That moved a hand and a foot." He glanced at John and said to the angel, "If I were writing this, I would say, 'Jesus took authority over the forces of salvation. He took authority over the planting and the harvesting. Abundant crops of faith will be upon the earth. He will sit upon his throne and wear His crown, and the church will be His bride.'"

"You may have that chance," replied the angel.

"Shall I help John?"

"Have you forgotten? He can neither hear you nor see you."

"I saw this in my dream," C.H. said excitedly to the angel. "A trumpet will sound, and the King will go to the white horse and put His brand on him. He will strengthen the rider and the horse with His own hand. The white horse will spawn many white horses, and they will gallop across the world."

He continued, getting even more excited. "There will come a great inundation, and fertile soil will be deposited across the face of the earth. Men will be given seed and told to sow the seeds of truth. The Gospel will be preached, and a vast community of the children of the evening will grow on earth. There will be seven years of bountiful harvests."

"Seven is symbolic," said the angel. "Do you know that?"

"Sure. We could be talking a thousand ... or something else, right?"

"The war will continue through both years of abundance and years of famine," said the angel.

"Yeah, and ugly cows will try to eat the fat cows. It's that Wormwood stuff," said C.H.

When the new King opened the second seal, the living creature with the face of an ox said, "Come," and a red horse stood before John. As the rider on the red horse rode away, C.H. thought he smelled blood, and he heard sounds of war and the clashing of weapons. Jesus took authority over the governments and kingdoms of the world.

When Jesus opened the third seal, the living creature with the face of a man, appearing as one who is exchanging goods and seeking profits, said, "Come," and a black horse stood before John. As the rider on the black horse rode away, C.H. thought he saw black dust swirling behind the horse. He gave the angel a quizzical look.

"Love of money," replied the angel.

Jesus opened the fourth seal and took authority over death. The living creature with the face of an eagle said, "Come," and a pale horse stood before John.

When an eagle soars, C.H. thought, *death is on the hunt.*

Jesus opened the fifth and sixth seals and took authority over the souls of the morning who had been sealed by God. He took authority over all souls who would ever live upon the earth.

Jesus took authority over the sun, the moon, and the stars. He took authority over the winds that blow. Joseph's second dream was consummated.

C.H. applauded. "You are right, Helper. What we have here are parallel stories."

He looked at John. Six seals had been opened, and John had written about Jesus having received all power and authority in heaven and on earth. "I guess that covers the *now* part," he said.

Jesus opened the seventh seal. At that moment a hush fell upon heaven. The singing and praying stopped, and all was quiet. There was a half hour of total silence in heaven.

C.H. felt like he had been there before. It was the same feeling he had when Joseph came home at noon to serve the meal to his brothers. From antiquity to a quiet moment in heaven, the long morning of God's creation was finally over. It was noon, and it was time for bread.

In the silence, C.H. wondered what might come next. He remembered something Jesus had said. "I have come to bring fire on the earth, and how I wish it were already kindled!" Luke 12:49 NIV

C.H. wondered what Jesus could have meant by that.

Finally, the half hour of silence in heaven ended, and in a flash seven angels stood before God. They were given seven trumpets, and they stood ready to sound them.

"Trumpets mean action," C.H. hollered. "It looks like the man from a far country is ready for action." He looked at John. "I hope he's ready to write, because we are about to see what will 'take place later.'" He remembered what Paul had said: "Again, if the trumpet does not sound a clear call, who will get ready for battle?" 1 Corinthians 14:8 NIV

Throughout history trumpets have been used by various groups and organizations to signal special events or sound calls for action. Some authorities say that the trumpet predates all other musical instruments and that it was first used in Egypt.

It is possible that Joseph used trumpets to assemble his workers and to signal them as they worked in the fields.

Using the trumpet as a mass media signal is a technique originally given by God. He told Moses to make two silver trumpets and to use them for signaling. The priests were to blow them, and trumpets would be used with varying signals to assemble people and indicate actions.

They were also to be used at times of rejoicing and at times of worship. God told Moses that the sounding of the trumpets was to be a lasting ordinance for future generations, that it would be a memorial for the people, and that He, God Himself, would hear them.

The seven angels stood ready to sound their trumpets. A war against a deadly plague of sin was raging, but there was a problem. C.H. sensed it, and he became greatly alarmed.

"The Bread of Heaven," he yelled. "There's no bread. Everyone will starve," cried C.H. "Even a ten-foot-tall Zuzim from Bashan cannot fight without bread."

C.H. pointed to the blazing torches and cried, "Only the Bread of Heaven can overcome the famine. All people are just like me. They are dead, and only the Bread of Heaven will save them."

He looked at the angels holding the trumpets. One of them appeared ready to sound his horn.

"Wait!" yelled C.H. "Don't sound a trumpet yet. Something is missing!" He looked at the person who had opened the seventh seal. "Oh, Jesus, please don't sound a trumpet yet. Remember Abraham? How about those disciples who are waiting and praying?" He braced himself to hear a trumpet sound. But no trumpet sounded.

Another angel came and stood at the altar. He was given much incense to offer. The angel held many prayers. He held the prayers of all the saints on the golden altar before the throne. He held the prayers of the little band of disciples waiting on earth. Smoke, incense, and prayers mingled and went up before God from the angel's hand.

C.H. looked at John, and he knew that John's heart was pounding. C.H. could not breathe, yet he prayed, "Keep the promise. Please keep the promise." He saw his prayers rise up from the angel's hand.

The throne was a fiery place. God Himself appeared as a raging fire. Flashes of lightning, rumblings, and peals of thunder came from the throne. Jesus' eyes flashed like the seven blazing torches.

Then it happened. The One who had received all power and authority in heaven and on earth sent the mighty angel to fulfill the long-awaited promise. The angel took the golden censer, filled it with fire from the altar, and hurled it upon the earth. And there came peals of thunder, rumblings, flashes of lightning, and an earthquake.

God's life-giving Spirit arrived on earth for the first time. *Pneuma,* the Greek word for Spirit in the New Testament, about which Jesus spoke, had finally arrived.

After so many years the Bread of Heaven was poured out. What an event! It separated the living from the dead. It stood between the faithful and the plague. Men had waited for it since the days of creation. For the first time there was the merging of the immortal with the mortal. Mortality took on immortality. A new age was born, and like Jacob holding on to Esau's heel, it came holding on to the age that was past.

"Hallelujah! Hallelujah!" said C.H., raising his hands high above his head.

The angel said, "Follow me."

In a blink C.H. found himself sitting in a house with some people. It was the day of Pentecost. A sound like the blowing of a violent wind came from heaven and filled the whole house.

He saw what appeared to be flames of fire that separated and came to rest on each of the people. They were all filled with the Holy Spirit and began to speak in other tongues as the Spirit enabled them.

C.H. was surprised at the great diversity of the people. There were representatives of many races, cultures, and languages.

The Spirit enabled those who received it to discern spiritual matters. A flame of fire appeared over Peter's head, and his mind was opened. He stood up and told them how Jesus had kept the promise. He said, "Exalted to the right hand of God, he has received from the Father the promised Holy Spirit and has poured out what you now see and hear." Acts 2:33 NIV

The wait was long, but the promise was faithful. God kept His promises to Abraham. The prophecies of Joel came true. The prophecies of Jeremiah came true. Joseph and Benjamin returned from the land of the dead, and Rachel ceased weeping in Ramah.

Jesus' promise to His disciples was kept. The symbolic story portrayed by grain in Egypt was consummated. Joseph's second dream came true. It all happened in one hour.

For the first time since God made a creature in His image, the life-giving Spirit of God was given to men in a family way. God started a family. He would have many sons and Jesus would have many brothers.

The arrival of Living Water was the beginning of sanctification. Those who were being justified by faith could now, at long last, also be sanctified by the Spirit. Those who were being baptized could now also receive the gift of the Holy Spirit.

Jesus explained God's biology when he said, "Flesh gives birth to flesh, but the Spirit gives birth to spirit." John 3:6 NIV

While the gift of the Spirit is only a deposit, it is the earnest of something greater, and it comes with a promise. It comes as a living entity and as a progenitor of life. It comes directly from God, and it carries the genetic properties of His Person. "Spirit gives life." John 6:63 NIV

The Greek word for "Spirit" found in the New Testament is the gender neutral word *pneuma.* It is neither male nor female.

On the day of Pentecost a unique thing happened. *Pneuma,* the "wind" or "breath," sired children for God who are neither male nor female. Christians are actually a different species from the water-bound creatures that came from Adam. Christ was the firstborn of a new type: real children of God.

Nothing is more wonderful than that free gift of the Holy Spirit! It is the gift that expresses His love and gives birth to His children. It is a private thing between God and the person to whom it is given.

Peter preached, "Repent and be baptized, every one of you, in the name of Jesus Christ for the forgiveness of your sins. And you will receive the gift of the Holy Spirit." Acts 2:38 NIV

C.H. watched people being convicted of their sins and confessing their faith that Jesus is the Son of God. Long lines of people formed near the water where the apostles had led them. They went down into the water one at a time and were baptized. C.H. could hear the words. The baptizing person would say, "I baptize you in the name of the Father, the Son, and the Holy Spirit."

"I get it," said C.H. as he watched people being baptized. "This is the first generation that will not pass away. If their boat capsizes, it won't matter because they won't die."

"I want that," he said as he got in line to be baptized. "Bread, at last."

"What are you doing?" asked the angel.

"I'm gonna be christened with a new name," said C.H.

"Have you forgotten that you are a dead man?" asked the angel. "Baptizing the dead is of no avail."

"But this is such an opportunity," said C.H. "I could be baptized by Peter."

"You will have other opportunities," said the angel. "Because the Lord God has answered your prayer. You may return to your body now, and you will no longer be a dead man."

C.H. instantly returned to his body. Though his out-of-body trip had been long, his life-threatening episode on the banks of Lynx Lake had been short. All things are possible with God.

He awoke in the hospital and felt pain in his resuscitated body.

A nurse walked in and said, "You're awake! How do you feel?"

"Lousy," he grumbled.

At that moment an attractive olive-skinned girl came into the hospital room.

"Oh, good," the nurse said to the girl. "You have come to see the results of your good work."

The nurse turned to C.H. and said, "Would you like to meet the paramedic who saved your life? She gave you mouth-to-mouth resuscitation."

The nurse faced the olive-skinned girl. "Mr. Roland, this is Miss Sharee."

"Hello, Mr. Roland," said Miss Sharee. "It is nice to meet you."

The nurse excused herself and hurried out of the room to help another patient.

"Thanks for blowing some air into me, Miss Sharee," C.H. said.

The girl blushed slightly, making her look even more beautiful. "You may call me by my real name," she said. "It's Isis."

C.H. did a quick double-take. She was beautiful, and he could see a tiny tattoo on her upper arm peeking out below her sleeve.

Thank You, Lord! C.H. prayed silently. *For everything.*

Printed in the United States
44475LVS00005B/1-60